CATWOMAN™
THE JUNIOR NOVEL

HERE KITTY KITTY

WARNER BROS. PICTURES PRESENTS

IN ASSOCIATION WITH VILLAGE ROADSHOW PICTURES A DI NOVI PICTURES PRODUCTION HALLE BERRY "CATWOMAN" BENJAMIN BRATT LAMBERT WILSON FRANCES CONROY AND SHARON STONE
MUSIC BY KLAUS BADELT EXECUTIVE PRODUCERS MICHAEL FOTTRELL BENJAMIN MELNIKER MICHAEL E. USLAN ROBERT KIRBY AND BRUCE BERMAN BASED ON CHARACTERS CREATED BY BOB KANE AND PUBLISHED BY DC COMICS
STORY BY THERESA REBECK AND JOHN BRANCATO & MICHAEL FERRIS SCREENPLAY BY JOHN BRANCATO & MICHAEL FERRIS AND JOHN ROGERS PRODUCED BY DENISE DI NOVI ED McDONNELL
VILLAGE ROADSHOW PICTURES   www.catwoman.com   America Online Keyword: Catwoman   DIRECTED BY PITOF   WARNER BROS. PICTURES

Book design by Joe Merkel

1 2 3 4 5 6 7 8 9 10

❖

First Edition
www.harperchildrens.com

CATWOMAN™

THE·JUNIOR·NOVEL

Adapted by

JASMINE JONES

Screenplay by

JOHN ROGERS AND
MIKE FERRIS & JOHN BRANCATO

HarperEntertainment

An Imprint of HarperCollinsPublishers

Chapter One

Thump, thump, thump, thump, thump.

Electronic music blared across the alley, directly into Patience Philips's skull . . . or so it seemed to Patience. She buried her head beneath her pillow, but even the heavy down wasn't enough to muffle the noise. Patience groaned and yanked the pillow off her head. She glanced at the clock. Four o'clock in the morning. She had been struggling to fall asleep for six hours—and there were only two hours left until she would have to get up and go to work....

Why today, of all days? Patience wondered as she stumbled out of bed, tangling herself in the blankets. Giving the sheets a violent kick, she tripped across the floor of her clean, tidy studio apartment to the window and peered out. The party across the alley was in full swing. Patience's neighbor was in the center of the action, dancing and laughing. *I guess he thinks he's a pretty cool dude*, Patience thought, feeling about as un-cool as humanly possible. Patience sighed and shook her head. *How can these people be out so late on a weeknight?* she wondered. *Don't they have jobs?*

Patience bit her lip, hesitating. She hated to be a pest, but she really needed her sleep. Wearily, Patience yanked open her window. "Hello?" she called across the alley. "Excuse me? If you could just . . . ?" Patience didn't bother finishing her question—no one had heard her, anyway. *Besides,* Patience thought as she peered in at the party, *why would they turn the music down for me? They're having a blast.*

A meow cut through Patience's thoughts, and she looked down into the courtyard where her irritating neighbor's sleek motorcycle was parked. An enormous dark-spotted gray-and-black cat was sitting on the seat, watching her with intense golden eyes. The cat had a scarab-shaped mark on its forehead and was the largest cat Patience had ever seen.

Patience gave the cat a rueful grin. "At least someone's having fun," she called down to the cat. "Right?"

I just wish it were me, Patience thought as she stumbled back to bed.

Colors splashed across the canvas as the party music throbbed through the walls to Patience's apartment. It was dawn. Patience had given up on trying to sleep and had decided to let out her anger in the best way she knew how—by painting. Patience was a designer by day, but she was also a very talented artist. She dashed another stroke across the vibrant painting just as the music fell silent.

The party was over.

Patience heaved a sigh of relief. But a moment later, she heard a mournful yowl. Then another meow, which sounded as though it was coming from right outside her apartment.

Setting down her paintbrush, Patience lifted the window and looked outside.

The golden-eyed cat was clearly afraid to move, stuck on top of a cornice at the corner of Patience's building. It let out another pitiful meow.

"You again?" Patience said to the cat. "Are you stuck? How'd you . . . ?" Patience looked at the side of the wall. She wasn't sure how the cat could have reached the cornice—there seemed to be no way up or down. *There must be a way I can't see,* Patience told herself. *The cat didn't get up there by magic.* "Come on down, cat," Patience urged.

She reached for the cat, but it yowled and backed away.

"It's okay, I won't let you fall," Patience urged as she reached toward the cornice. But it was too far, and the cat seemed to know it, meowing in protest.

Looking down, Patience took a deep breath and crawled onto the windowsill. Her heart thudded in her chest as she clung to the side of the sill. *Why am I doing this?* Patience wondered

4

as she looked down. It was a long drop. Still, she felt compelled to help that cat. *Maybe it reminds me of a cat I used to know,* Patience reasoned as she balanced herself on the windowsill. *Not that I've known many cats.* Patience had never had a pet in her life.

Suddenly, a loud roar echoed across the alley. Patience lost her balance, and clung more tightly to the windowsill. She looked down to see Cool Dude, her partying neighbor, zooming away on his motorcycle. "I thought 'party all night' was a figure of speech," Patience said dryly. "Have a nice day!" she called after Cool Dude. Not that he heard her over the scream of his motorcycle.

Frowning, Patience reached for the cat. "C'mon, now," she urged. "I'm sleep-deprived. Work with me."

The cat didn't move.

This is turning into a very annoying day, Patience thought. She looked around, hoping to see a ledge that would get her closer to the cat. Sure enough, there was an air conditioner sticking out of the window in the apartment next to hers. Patience stepped on it gingerly. *It seems secure,* Patience thought as she slowly stood on it, hugging the wall. She reached for the cat....

"Hey!" called a voice from the street below. "Hold on! Don't you move!"

Patience looked down at the tall, slim man with dark hair who was calling to her. His car was haphazardly parked behind him, the driver's door still open.

"Whatever you're thinking, whatever you're feeling, it's not worth it, understand?" The man went on, his voice gentler now. "I'm a cop. Maybe I can help."

He thinks I'm trying to jump out of the window, Patience realized. It was almost funny, but Patience didn't dare laugh—she might lose her balance. She didn't even dare speak too much. "No, thank you," she grunted as politely as she could. "I'm fine. It's just..."

"We're going to get through this together. You and me. What's your name?" the man called.

Patience looked back up at the cornice. The golden-eyed cat had disappeared. *Where did it go?* Patience wondered in confusion. Only a minute ago, it had seemed to have nowhere to leap to. "Patience Philips," she said to the man below, "but the cat..."

"Sure, Patience," the man said slowly. "It's a beauty, real cute—"

Patience had to keep herself from grunting in frustration. *This guy clearly thinks I'm nuts,* she realized. "The cat's not here anymore," she explained.

"And I know that makes you very sad."

I give up, Patience thought. "Right." She turned back toward her apartment. But when she tried to crawl back to her window, the air conditioner wobbled, pitching her off balance. Patience let out a small cry. Flailing, she grabbed the cornice to steady herself.

"What's your apartment number?" the man shouted.

Patience clung to the cornice. "Twenty-three!"

The man darted into the building as the air conditioner tilted dangerously. *Creak*. The bolts groaned, threatening to pull free from the side of the building. *Hurry, hurry*, Patience thought.

A moment later, there was a loud crash as the man burst into her apartment. The air conditioner shifted again, and Patience slipped, tripping on the ledge in front of her window. She started to fall.

Just then, the cop leaned through the window and grabbed Patience around the waist. Her body leaned back over his arm, as though she was his partner in a midair tango. Patience felt her heart plunge with fear. His grip was the only thing keeping her from falling.

"Help," Patience whispered.

"I've got you," the man assured her. "I've got you."

Patience scrambled against the brick wall in her stockinged feet as the man strained to haul her in through the window. Muscles and tendons stood out on his arm as he hoisted Patience inside quickly, sending them both tumbling to the floor.

"Close call," the man said, gasping.

Patience drew air into her lungs as relief flooded her body. She looked into the man's face. "Thank you," she breathed. Now that she was finally safe, she realized that her rescuer was actually very handsome—and that there was kindness in the depths of his dark eyes.

Oh my gosh, what am I doing? Patience thought suddenly. *I'm lying on top of a strange man!* She scrambled to her feet.

"You okay?" the man asked as he stood up, straightening his clothes.

"Fine," Patience said quickly, feeling her face burning. "Never better. You?" *Oh, that's great, Patience*, she told herself harshly. *Nice conversational opening for the man who just saved your life.*

"I'm fine," the cop replied automatically. "But..."

Patience and the man stared at each other for a moment. *He wants to know why I was standing on the windowsill*, Patience thought. *How can I tell him that I went out there to rescue a cat that disappeared?*

Almost as though it had heard her thoughts, the golden-eyed cat chose that moment to stalk through the window and hop lightly to the floor. It gave a languorous stretch, meowed, and then darted through Patience's open apartment door.

Patience looked at the cop. "That was the cat."

The man lifted his eyebrows. "You weren't kidding. You climbed out there to rescue your *cat*?"

Okay, when he puts it that way, it sounds completely loony, Patience thought. "No," she said quickly. "I mean yes, but it's not *mine*."

The cop's expression changed, and Patience thought she saw a measure of respect in his dark eyes. "You climbed out there to rescue somebody else's cat. That's . . . something else."

"Why?" Patience asked. "You came out to rescue *me*."

She smiled at the man, and he smiled back, flashing a set of white, even teeth. Something in the way the man was looking at her made her feel shy, and she had to look away. She glanced at her watch. "Oh, no," Patience cried when she saw the time. "I'm going to be late. I've got to go." Patience raced to her drafting table and grabbed the designs she had slaved over for the past four weeks.

"But—"

"I've got this big presentation," Patience explained as she and the man stepped into the hall.

"Oh," the man said. "Well. Good luck with that—"

"Thank you!" Patience turned toward the door and noticed that the lock was damaged. *Of course,* Patience realized. *The cop had to break it when he burst into my apartment to save me.*

The cop pulled shut the door. "It'll hold," he said, eyeing the lock.

"Thanks again!" Patience said eagerly. She felt she should say more, but didn't know what to add.

"*Go,*" the man commanded.

Patience smiled and darted away. She bit her lip as her purse fell to the floor and skidded a few feet, but she managed to scoop it up and race off.

The cop watched her go for a moment, then

tested the door once more to make sure it was okay. Looking down, he spotted a wallet lying on the ground near where Patience's purse had fallen. The corners of his mouth curled into a smile as he picked it up.

This is turning into a very interesting day, he thought.

Chapter Two

Patience hurried into the lobby of the Hedare building—world headquarters for Hedare Beauty, the leading cosmetics brand in the United States. The sleek lobby was decorated in marble and glass, and the walls were covered in plasma screens displaying the perfect profile of Laurel Hedare—the wife of the company's founder—whose fine features, short blond hair, and ice-blue eyes made up the face of the company.

Patience shoved open the door with her hip, then rushed into the lobby. "Sorry!" she said as she bumped into someone. She backed away, running into someone else, and had to mutter another apology.

Patience sighed. Things at the office were already not going well.

George Hedare paced the width of the boardroom as his wife, Laurel, gazed at him impassively from her place at the end of the long conference table. George was a commanding presence, made all the more so by the fact that he had built Hedare Beauty from a small operation into a world enterprise. And now the company had developed something that was going to change the face of the industry. "Hedare Beauty stands at the threshold of a new era," George Hedare announced as he gestured to a plasma screen that showed two dramatic photos of the same woman. In the first photo, she looked haggard and old. In the second, her skin was smooth and seemed to glow—she looked twenty years younger. "Botox, collagen, dermabrasion . . ." Hedare went on. "Women will suffer for beauty. We also know they'll pay for it. Our goal, of course, is that they pay us."

The members of the board chuckled.

Everyone except for Laurel, that is, who gazed at her husband in stony silence.

"And soon that will be more true than it has ever been," Hedare said, ignoring his wife's glare. "In one week, we will launch the most exciting product to hit the beauty industry since soap: Beau-line. It doesn't just hide the effects of aging . . . it *reverses* them." He gestured toward the images on the plasma screen, and the room burst into applause.

"However," Hedare went on, his voice softening slightly, "with change comes sacrifice. As we move into the future, we must set aside the past."

Laurel pushed back her chair and slowly rose from her seat. "My husband . . . and I . . . have decided it's time for me to step aside as the face of Hedare," she announced. "It has been a magnificent fifteen years, but we have chosen a new face to represent Beau-line. A . . . younger face."

A murmur of surprise rippled through the room as Laurel took her seat. The image on the plasma screen shifted to reveal a beautiful young woman with dark skin, lush dark hair, and exotic almond-shaped eyes. The Beau-line slogan, "To Be More," appeared below the model's image.

"Drina!" Hedare announced. "The future of Hedare Beauty. I look forward to seeing you all at the gala, where you can toast her and our success in person."

"Careful, George," Laurel quipped, "she's not old enough to drink."

This time it was Hedare who glared in stony silence as laughter filled the room. Laurel gave him a brittle smile.

She always did like to have the last laugh.

"Don't be intimidated," Patience's good friend, Sally, coached as she walked Patience to Hedare's office for her presentation. "You've got more talent than anybody in the building. Don't hide your light under a bushel." Sally paused, adding, "Whatever that means."

Patience didn't laugh—she was too nervous. "It's just—this is my first lead campaign, Sally.

I want everything to be perfect, you know?"

Patience managed a thin smile as she paused in front of Hedare's door. Just then, muffled shouts sounded from behind the door. Patience flinched.

Sally grimaced. "Eesh," she said. "Good luck."

I'm going to need it, Patience thought as she knocked on the door.

"Come in!" Hedare bellowed.

Taking a deep breath, Patience put her hand on the doorknob, turned it, and peered into the office. Hedare was seated behind his desk, and Laurel gazed out the window in silence as Patience walked into the room. "Mr. Hedare," Patience said awkwardly. "Hi."

Hedare didn't reply.

Maybe I should come back later, Patience thought. "Did you still want me to—"

"Sit," Hedare commanded.

Patience sat, trying hard to quiet the squirmy butterflies in her stomach.

"Philips," Hedare growled, "I'm not pleased." He glanced down at Patience's designs for the

Beau-line campaign. "That's not even close to what I wanted. I can't imagine what you were thinking."

Patience was stunned. She had thought that the campaign was her best work—the freshest design the company had ever seen. *How could I have been so wrong?* she wondered. "I'm so sorry, I—"

"Look at this red," Hedare went on. "It's all wrong. I wanted something darker—"

"But you said specifically—" Patience bit off the words. She knew there was no point in arguing with the boss.

Hedare glared at her. *"I know what I said."*

His words hit her like a slap to the face. "Maybe I misunderstood," Patience corrected.

"Clearly."

"Mr. Hedare, I'm so sorry," Patience said quickly. "I can fix it. If you'll just give me another chance—"

"I don't reward incompetence. I have no idea why I expected your art to show better taste than your wardrobe."

Patience felt her cheeks burning.

Hedare shook his head, looking at Patience disdainfully. "And try a manicure."

"Oh, for God's sake, George," Laurel broke in, turning from the window, "Let her fix it. You change your mind every hour. It's good and you know it."

Hedare opened his mouth to say something, then seemed to change his mind. He turned back to Patience. "By midnight, tonight."

Hedare looked down at the papers on his desk as Patience stood to leave. *Clearly, the meeting is over,* Patience thought. She gave Laurel a grateful smile before hurrying out of the office.

Now I've been rescued twice in one day, Patience thought as she scurried out the door. *I guess you could say I'm one lucky girl.*

Patience stood in front of the ladies' room mirror, inhaling deeply. It wasn't really working —her nerves were shot. *That was the worst meeting of my entire life,* Patience thought as she took another breath. *And I can inhale and*

exhale all I want—nothing is going to change what happened.

Just then, Patience heard someone walk into the ladies' room. She looked up.

"If you ask me," Laurel said as she checked her makeup in the mirror, "I think you look fabulous."

Patience looked down at her outfit. It didn't exactly scream, "Look at me!"

"Maybe he's right," Patience admitted, giving Laurel a wan smile. "I am a little—"

"Making other people feel small is his game," Laurel interrupted. "You can't win, so you have to refuse to play."

The words held the ring of truth. Still, they were hard for Patience to accept. "I really thought I knew what he wanted," she said miserably.

"Don't feel too bad, honey," Laurel said gently. "I thought I did, too." She gave Patience a smile. "Hang in there."

Patience leaned over her drafting table, transforming the Beau-line logo while Sally stood behind her, digging in her purse. Looking up, Patience caught a glimpse of the unmarked jar as Sally pulled it out.

Patience frowned. "You know, you're addicted to that stuff."

"Happily," Sally admitted. "Beau-line is magic in a bottle."

"How do you keep getting it? Production doesn't even start until tomorrow."

Sally didn't answer—she was busy spreading the salve under her eyes. She held the jar out to Patience, who waved it off. "No, thanks."

Sally shrugged. "Well, some of us need more help than others." She winced suddenly and shook her head.

Patience lifted her eyebrows at her friend.

"Headaches again," Sally admitted. "My brain's all...cranky."

Patience grinned. That was the thing about Sally—she could always make Patience smile.

"Man sandwich," Lance, another one of Patience's coworkers, said as he poked his head into Patience's cubicle, "twelve o'clock."

Lance hurried off as Sally peered into the hall.

"Oh, my God." She gasped. "Let it be me, let it be me...."

Patience looked up and was surprised to see the cop who had rescued her that morning.

"Hello," he said as he walked into Patience's workstation.

"Hi," Patience said shyly as she stood to greet him. "Sally, this is..." Patience paused, realizing that she didn't know the man's name. "The detective I told you about...from this morning."

"Tom Lone," the cop said, holding out his hand.

"That is such a good name," Sally gushed as she shook his hand. "Tom Lone. Rhymes with phone, bone, cone—not that rhyming's all that important—" Sally lifted her eyebrows at Patience, who was flashing her a You Can Go Now look. "Um. I'll be over here. In my cubicle. Alone," Sally added, stressing the rhyme. She disappeared into the workstation next door.

"So," Patience said brightly. "Hi. How did you know where to—?"

"You dropped something," Lone said, holding out a very familiar-looking wallet. "You can really cover ground when you're in a hurry," he added, smiling.

Patience took the wallet gratefully as Lone looked around her cubicle. He gestured toward one of the drawings in Patience's sketchbook, which was propped open at the back of her drafting table. "This is nice."

"You think?" Patience was flattered that he had chosen to compliment her on her original work, rather than the sketches of products and labels that littered her cubicle.

"Reminds me of early Chagall," Lone said, nodding knowingly. "Elegant, but whimsical. Very much in the old Dutch Masters tradition. The old Masters. Who were Dutch . . ." His voice trailed off.

Patience had to laugh. Lone sounded as though he were reading from a catalog at the Metropolitan Museum of Art. A seriously whacked-out catalog.

"I'm . . . impressed?" she said, not wanting to point out that Chagall wasn't exactly Dutch.

"Don't be," Lone confessed, grinning. "I saw all the art in your apartment, so I Googled it at the office, and just between you and me? I thought Dutch Masters was a cigar my lieutenant used to smoke. But really, I like it," he added, looking back toward Patience's work. "A lot."

"Thank you." Patience could feel the blood rising to her cheeks. She didn't know what to say. A loud thump came from Sally's side of the cubicle.

"I was hoping we could have a cup of coffee," Lone finished finally. "There's this Italian place right around the corner. Grecio's. On sixth."

Say "I'd love to," Patience commanded herself. *Say, "I can't wait."* But she just couldn't seem to make the words come out of her mouth.

"How about tomorrow? One o'clock?" Lone suggested.

Patience stood there in silence for a moment before she could finally force her mouth to move. "That . . . that sounds great," she managed.

A relieved smile spread across Lone's face. "Okay," he said brightly. "Tomorrow, then."

Patience smiled and nodded.

"You'll make sure she gets there, right?"

Lone asked Sally, who had just popped her head over the cubicle wall. "I'm counting on you."

"Yes, officer," Sally said, giving him a snappy salute. "Captain. Generalissimo. Sir."

Lone flashed Patience another megawatt grin and strode off down the hall.

Sally heaved a dreamy sigh as she watched him go, then turned to Patience. "Patience, he *so* likes you!" she said happily. "Okay, don't eat today, only water, and wear the leather outfit I got you for your birthday—"

"Hello?" Lance's voice called from his cubicle on the other side of Sally's.

"Lance would like me to remind you that he pitched in for the leather," Sally added.

Patience smiled and shook her head. Sally was always full of 'dating advice,' most of which would have made Patience feel like a complete idiot if she ever took it, which she never did. "A," Patience said, "it's just coffee. And B, never." *Not in my lifetime,* Patience thought, remembering the skintight pants and jacket.

That just wasn't her style.

Chapter Three

Patience spent the rest of the day working on the Beau-line designs. She was so absorbed by her work that she didn't even notice as, one by one, the other designers in her department switched off their lights and went home.

At eleven-thirty, Patience shoved her design boards into her large leather portfolio with one hand while she used the other to dial the mailroom. But the manager explained that all of the couriers had gone home. Patience would have to deliver the designs to Hedare personally. She just hoped she wasn't too late.

Patience took a cab to the Hedare factory, and walked into the complex hauling the heavy portfolio. She tried the door to the printing building, but it was locked. Patience checked her watch. She was late. Late—*and fired!* she thought, pounding on the door. "Hello?" she called. "Anyone?" There was no reply. Looking around, Patience saw that there were lights coming from another section of the factory— research and development. *Maybe I can get in through there*, Patience thought. She hurried around to the back and found an open door. Breathing a sigh of relief, Patience hurried inside.

Patience had been to the Hedare factory complex before, but never to this section. She needed the printing division, but wasn't sure how to get there from where she was. A chill skittered down her spine as she looked around at the brooding walls lined with a spiderweb of dark pipes. Silence seemed to fill the space around her. A dim light shone from around a corner, and Patience hurried toward it.

"I don't care that the FDA never saw the headaches, the nausea, or fainting spells. Those are symptoms I can live with." Dr. Slavicky, the head of Hedare research and development, said to the figure half-hidden in the shadows of his office. The only light came from video screens, which displayed moving bacteria magnified by an electron microscope. "And with what we stand to make from consumers demanding their fix, I can live with it being addictive. But these side effects from the long-term studies . . ." Behind him, the images on the monitors shifted to show images of women, the skin dripping from their faces like molten wax. "I can't live with turning people into monsters—"

The figure in the shadows murmured softly.

"I thought I could live with it . . ." Slavicky said, shaking his head, "but I'm . . . not sure any-more. . . ."

Out in the hallway, Patience heard low voices from down the hall. *Great*, she thought, relief flooding her body, *now I can ask someone for directions*. Spotting a half-open door, Patience pushed it open gently and stepped inside.

Patience walked cautiously into the lab and looked around. *What is that?* she wondered, spying the monitor. On the screen, a computer image of a woman's face was changing. The face was old, lined with fine wrinkles, but slowly it began to morph, becoming younger and firmer. But the change went on, and after a moment, the face became hard, stony, and almost skeletal....

Patience backed away from the image, slamming into a table behind her.

"Who's there?" Slavicky barked.

Patience was sure she had seen something she wasn't supposed to. She didn't reply. She just ran.

As Patience fled, the door at the end of the hall began to open. She froze, ducking back around the corner.

A man stepped through the door as another emerged from the lab. Patience knew who they were—Armando and Wesley—George Hedare's assistants . . . and bodyguards. She hurried away from them.

Wesley joined Armando, and the two men followed the sound of Patience's footsteps.

Patience found her way into a large production

area. She ducked behind some machinery, her back to a vat.

"Come on out," Wesley called. "It's okay. We'd just like to ask you a few questions."

Breathing a sigh of relief, Patience stepped out from her hiding place. "I'm sorry. I think I'm in the wrong—"

Bang!

A bullet sliced through the air, slamming into the vat of Hedare cosmetics just beside her head. Without thinking, Patience dropped her portfolio and ran.

She ran blindly, not knowing where she was headed, desperate for a way out. Bullets flew as she raced down a metal ramp. *Please, please, let me out of here,* Patience begged silently as she darted into a waste treatment area.

A maze of metal catwalks wound over a pool of dark water. Patience could hear rushing liquid and waste chemicals pouring through the web of pipes overhead. Patience's heart thudded in fear as she faced several enormous pipes that led away from the treatment area. Patience had no choice—there was no other way out.

She picked one and ducked inside.

Patience scurried through the pipe, dodging as air whooshed past her. Putting out her hands to steady herself, she stumbled forward . . . until the pipe suddenly ended.

Below, there was nothing but a long plunge to a raging river below. Gasping, Patience turned back, but she didn't get far. A tidal wave roared toward her. They had flooded the pipes. There was no time to react as the massive wall of water crashed over her, sweeping her over the edge.

And then everything went black.

Patience woke up to the sound of her phone ringing. She sat up . . .

. . . and fell off the top of her bookcase.

Patience blinked. *What happened? Why was I on top of the bookcase?* she thought groggily, suddenly realizing that her muscles were stiff, and her muddy clothes from the night before were strewn all over the apartment.

Patience's machine answered the phone.

"Patience, where are you?" Sally's worried voice said into the machine. "Hedare is on the warpath. And Tom called. He says you never showed up for your date."

Feeling dazed, Patience glanced at the clock. 1:50 P.M. Patience read the numbers through a thick fog. They didn't make any sense. *This is morning . . . isn't it?* she wondered. *Is it early morning?* But Sally's concerned voice snapped her back to reality—no, it wasn't morning. It was late—super late! Patience leaped to her feet, unable to believe that she had been asleep for so long.

"Look, I'm really worried," Sally went on. "Please call me. What's going on? What happened?"

Sally's voice was cut off by a beep.

"I...I don't know," Patience said to the empty room. "I don't remember. . . ." She glanced up at the window. It was broken. Glass was strewn beneath it. "What happened?" Patience asked aloud.

A meow cut through the room.

Patience looked over to see the golden-eyed

cat, eyeing her coolly from the top of her dresser. Innocently, it began to lick a paw.

"You," Patience said. She walked toward the cat, and tentatively stroked its fur from its forehead all the way down its back. "Did you . . . did you do all this?" There was something about this cat—Patience could almost believe that it had broken into her home and made a mess of her apartment all by itself.

Reaching out, Patience checked the tag on its collar. "You're freaking me out, kitty," she told the cat slowly, her hands shaking. "You've got to go home. Now."

The cozy wood-frame house was nestled among a concrete jungle of high-rise apartment buildings. Patience double-checked the number just as the front door opened.

"Are you Ophelia Powers?" Patience asked. "I got your cat off a ledge. Now it won't leave me alone." She held out the cat to the woman, who looked to be in her mid-fifties.

Ophelia didn't take the cat. She studied

Patience's face for a moment, then said, "I think you should come in."

Patience hesitated. "Oh, I can't. I'm sorry. Thank you, but I'm late for work, and I..." Her voice trailed off. Ophelia had already turned and walked back into the house, leaving Patience holding the cat.

Sighing, Patience stepped through the door and found her way into a cluttered living room crowded with cats. Several of them swarmed around Patience, nudging her ankles and rubbing against her legs, as she took a seat on the couch. Ophelia brought them each a cup of tea, and Patience tried to gently shove away the adoring felines while the golden-eyed cat eyed her regally from the back of the couch.

Ophelia sat down across from her. Patience had so many questions, she wasn't sure where to begin.

"Midnight," Ophelia said.

"I'm sorry? What?"

Ophelia's eyes flicked to the golden-eyed cat. "Her name. She's an Egyptian Mau, a rare breed.

Temple cats. Said to have special powers."

"Right," Patience said in a wry voice. "Like popping out of nowhere and scaring people half to death?"

A smile twitched at Ophelia's lips. "Among other things."

"This has been a terrible day already." Patience shook her head. "And I can't even remember most of yesterday. And every time I turn around, your cat is . . ." Patience stopped herself. "I'm sorry, this isn't your problem. I don't even know why I'm telling you, it's just—"

"It's all right," Ophelia said gently. "Tell me. Please."

Patience hesitated. *There's something odd about this woman,* she thought. Patience somehow felt that Ophelia would understand what she had been going through. But there just wasn't time to get into it. "I'm sorry. I can't. I've got to get to work. I am *really* late."

"Then I think you should come back," Ophelia said with finality. "Anytime. I'm always here." Just then, she swatted at a calico cat that was lapping up Patience's tea. "Socrates! No caffeine." Ophelia looked up at Patience. "It makes him irritable."

Patience smiled and stood up. She wasn't sure how she was going to explain why she was six hours late for work, but she knew that it was time to face the music.

Wordlessly, Ophelia took a small wooden box from the table in front of her. Lifting the lid, she pulled out a molded ball of green herbs and tossed it at Patience.

Without thinking, Patience caught the ball and brought it to her nose, inhaling deeply. A soothing sense of calm swept over her, and Patience shuddered in relief.

Ophelia stared at Patience, her eyes wide. "Catnip," she said.

As if that explained everything.

"What is *wrong* with you?" Hedare had been bellowing at Patience from the moment she reached her desk. "You never delivered the designs. You do not, in fact, even know where they are. And you do not know where they are because, and I quote, 'I can't remember'? Your incompetence is staggering—"

Patience, who had been scribbling in a note-book, glanced up at her boss. "Hmm?"

Hedare looked as though he was about to burst a blood vessel. "Are you even listening to me?"

"Not as much as you're listening to yourself," Patience snapped.

Hedare snatched the top page out of Patience's notebook, and his expression grew dark at what he saw. It was a nasty caricature of him—smoke and fire spewing from his head. Hedare crumpled the paper in silent fury, then turned on his heel and stalked off.

A cold wave of fear washed over Patience. *What have I done?* she thought dizzily. She hadn't meant to be rude. She honestly didn't even know how it happened. It was like someone else had temporarily taken over her body. "Mr. Hedare, wait," she called sincerely. "I don't know what got into me. I'm sorry."

Hedare turned to face her, his eyes like

daggers. "Sorry? Is that all? 'Sorry' isn't nearly enough."

In a flash, that other person in Patience's body resurfaced, and Patience narrowed her eyes. "Then let me try the remix," she demanded in a deep growl. Patience could feel the entire art department watching her, but she didn't care. In fact, she *wanted* them to hear. "I'm sorry for every minute of my life I've wasted working for an untalented, unethical, and unappreciative egomaniac like you."

Hedare eyed her coldly. "Clean out your cubicle," he said before he walked away.

Suddenly, Patience felt her mind clear. *What just happened?* she thought desperately. "Wait!" she shouted. "Mr. Hedare!"

Hedare didn't stop.

"I didn't mean—Mr. Hedare! I was kidding!" Patience stopped in her tracks, and whispered, "Wasn't I?"

Sally came and stood next to Patience as she leaned against a cubicle wall, exhausted and confused.

Sally grinned. "My hero," she said.

Chapter Four

"I don't know how to describe it," Patience told Sally as they walked away from the Hedare building. "It's like ... it's like I was saying it, but I wasn't saying it at the same time."

"Well, whoever said it deserves the thanks of a grateful art department."

"You don't *understand*, Sally," Patience said, a cold fist of fear tightening in her stomach. "I wanted to hurt him. I would have liked hurting him."

Ruff! Ruff! Grr!

Two dogs strained at their leashes, barking madly as Patience and Sally walked past. Sally jumped back, but Patience stood her ground ... and hissed.

Sally lifted her eyebrows. "What was that?"

I don't know, Patience thought. She gave a little sniff. "Nothing," she said innocently. "Allergies?" At that moment, a glimmer in a nearby jewelry store window caught Patience's eye. She gazed at the display. At the center was a diamond-tipped claw necklace. The jewels were brilliant against black velvet. "Pretty..." Patience said huskily. "*Sooo* pretty..."

Sally didn't say anything.

"Sal?" Patience said, coming back to herself. She turned just in time to see Sally collapse. "Sally!"

"Have you noticed that when they keep you for observation, nobody ever observes you?" Sally asked dryly as an orderly rolled her down the hall on a gurney.

"Sal," Patience said quietly, "Do they know what's wrong with you?"

Sally shook her head. "Not a clue. They keep running tests, but..." Her voice trailed off. "But there is an upside," she added with a sly smile. "You should see my doctor."

Patience grinned. "It sounds like you're getting better already."

"Which reminds me—what's up with the handsome yet modest but who cares because he's so handsome detective?"

Patience knew her friend was hoping for juicy details, but she had to tell the truth. "Trust me. I don't think it's going to work out."

"You never think it's going to work out," Sally huffed. "I will not let you sabotage a good thing."

"You talk a pretty mean game in that backless gown."

"My shoulder blades are my best feature," Sally quipped. "Look. If it's broke, fix it. Now get out of here. The hottie doctor's coming," she explained, fluffing her hair. "I need to look vulnerable."

"It's wrong." Lone said gravely. He looked his audience straight in the eye. "You can't just take something without paying for it."

The group of ten-year-olds stared at him seriously. Lone knew that he had this crowd in the palm of his hand. "There's no such thing as a little bit against the law," he went on. "It is or it isn't. When you steal, you're the bad guy."

"Can I see your gun?" a kid interrupted.

"No," Lone replied automatically. "And we don't like bad guys, do we? We like—"

"Is it loaded?" another kid asked.

"Yes. We like good guys," Lone went on. "You know what makes somebody—"

"Will you shoot it?" asked yet another kid.

"No. You know what makes somebody good?" Lone tried to change the subject, although he knew that this was probably a lost cause. Kids always loved asking about the gun.

Another kid piped up. "Can *I* shoot it?"

Lone sighed, but when he looked up, his breath caught in his throat. Patience was standing at the back of the room, a paper coffee cup in her hand. Lone wondered what she was doing there as he continued, "I'm not saying it's easy. I'm not saying that some people don't choose to be bad. But I want something different for you. I want you all to be good guys." Lone smiled. "Now let's go shoot some hoops."

With a cheer, the kids leaped up from their overstuffed floor cushions and ran for the exit.

Patience walked over to Lone. "Hi," she said shyly. "I called the station, and they said you might be here." Holding out a paper cup, she added, "You never got your coffee."

Lone looked down at the cup, which Patience had decorated with colored pens. "Sorry," it read. Lone accepted the coffee and the apology.

"Look, I'm sorry I was so . . . weird," Patience said awkwardly. "It was just one of those crazy days." *One of those days where you fall off the top of your bookcase, get fired, and hiss at passing dogs*, Patience added mentally, hardly daring to hope that Lone might understand. "Do you ever have days like that?"

"Not exactly," Lone confessed. "But this day? It just got better."

Patience smiled in relief and followed Lone out to the community center's playground. "You are a brave man, facing a mob like that,"

Patience joked, nodding at the group of ten-year-olds playing basketball nearby. "And with no back-up!"

Lone took a sip of coffee. "Most of the time I work alone."

"By choice?" Patience asked.

Lone gave her a rueful smile. "Yes. Theirs."

Patience laughed.

"I've had partners," Lone explained. "But it turns out I take my job a little too seriously."

"You know my friend Sally? That's what she always says about me," Patience confessed. "She says I'm 'fun-deficient.'"

"I don't believe that."

A basketball bounced their way and Patience caught it. She dribbled it lightly with catlike swats, once, twice. "I haven't played since I was a kid," Patience said, tossing the ball back to a kid.

Lone gestured toward the kid, who tossed the ball to him. Lone dribbled toward Patience. She gave him an uncertain smile.

"One-on-one?" the kid suggested. His friends looked over curiously.

"Who?" Lone asked innocently. "Me and her?"

"One-on-one!" the group of kids chanted. "One-on-one!"

Lone and Patience squared off. Lone lunged, but Patience feinted, dodging away from him, dribbling in her catlike way.

Lone went for the ball again and managed to steal it. Patience stalked the ball, almost slithering down court as Lone went for the shot. The moment the ball was free, Patience pounced. She went in for a lay-up, but Lone blocked her. With an enormous leap, Patience landed her knee against Lone's chest and slam-dunked the ball!

Patience knocked Lone over, landing on top of him and tumbling to the ground. She couldn't help smiling as Lone stared at her, clearly intrigued by her unusual style. *Sally was right*, Patience thought as she stood, looking into Lone's dark eyes, *it would have been a mistake to sabotage a good thing*.

Just then, a voice piped up from the rear of the playground, where the ten-year-olds had been watching the game. "Hey, can we have our ball back?"

Thump, thump, thump, thump, thump.

It was the middle of the night, and dance music was once again blasting from across the alley and directly into Patience's skull. Groaning, Patience hauled herself out of bed and over to the window. Same apartment, same host— different party. *Enough*, Patience thought.

"Keep it down over there!" Patience shouted at top volume. She was surprised at the intensity of her own voice—it even managed to drown out the music for a second.

A moment later, Cool Dude stuck his head out of his window. "Get a life!" he shouted back, sneering. He turned back to his party and the music doubled in volume.

Fuming, Patience glanced down into the courtyard...where Cool Dude's shiny motorcycle sat. It was almost as though the motorcycle was waiting for her. A wicked smile crept across Patience's face. "Get a bus pass," she hissed.

She grabbed the windowsill to climb out, but as she looked down, she noticed that she was still in her nightgown.

That wouldn't do at all.

Patience strode to her closet, shoved aside the clothes hanging there and reached for a gift box. Reaching up, Patience pulled out the box and lifted the lid. Inside was the leather outfit Lance and Sally had given her for her birthday—tight leather pants, boots, and a jacket.

Patience ripped off the tags with her teeth, then turned to the shelves near her drawing table. Grabbing art supplies and a pair of scissors, Patience stalked to her bathroom.

She stared at herself intently as she hacked at her long curly hair, leaving it in short spikes. What this outfit needs, Patience thought as she ran paint streaks through her hair, is a little color. Next, she lined her eyes with kohl, and painted her lips a deep red. Perfect.

Back at the window, Patience leaped gracefully to the courtyard below. The motorcycle gleamed silently in the moonlight. Patience slid onto the seat and kick-started the bike, bringing it to life with a roar.

"Time to . . . accessorize," Patience purred.

With a squeal of rubber on asphalt, Catwoman took off into the night.

Chapter Five

Catwoman drove recklessly through the streets, skillfully dodging traffic. She laughed into the breeze as the air whipped against her face. Patience had never had so much fun in her life.

Patience almost drove right past the jewelry store, but—remembering the beautiful diamond-tipped claw necklace—skidded to a stop just in time. *Something like that would really make this outfit work*, Catwoman thought as she thrust out the kickstand. *After all, diamonds are a cat's best friend*.

Just then, there was a flash of light, and the crash of breaking glass. Some people were robbing the store. Catwoman cocked her head. "Hey, no fair, that was *my* idea."

A heavyset thief was breaking glass display cases with the butt of his gun while another used a blowtorch on a locked steel case. Catwoman crept up behind one and blew in his ear. By the time the thief turned around, she had disappeared.

Another crook was upstairs, shoving jewels into a black bag. Silent as a shadow, Catwoman tugged at a piece of fabric beneath the bag, sliding both across the glass case. She slashed two eyeholes into the fabric and tied it around the upper half of her face.

In a single, fluid movement, Catwoman dropped behind the short thief. "Amateurs," she murmured. The thief froze for a moment. Then, apparently deciding that the voice had been his imagination, he went back to pulling jewelry from the displays. Catwoman toyed with him for a few moments, peering over his shoulder, moving close to him, but always slipping away before he caught a glimpse. "Idiot," Catwoman purred. "Look behind you."

The thief whirled, pointing his gun.

But Catwoman had disappeared.

The heavyset thief kept his gun in hand as he pulled a display out of the case. It was the diamond claw necklace. He glanced up for a moment, but when he looked back at the display, the necklace was gone.

A moment later, a movement caught his eye, and he turned to see Catwoman standing next to the tall thief. She was wearing the necklace. Catwoman gave him a friendly wave as the heavyset thief held up his gun.

"What are you *doing*?" the tall thief asked, pulling his own gun.

Just then, the short thief hurried down the staircase. "There's somebody—"

"What?" the tall thief shouted.

"You boys think you can just barge in here and take all these beautiful things that don't belong to you?" Catwoman demanded from the top of the mezzanine.

A second later, three guns were trained on her.

Catwoman grinned. "What a *purr*-fect idea."

Plaster rained down as all three thieves fired at Catwoman. But she was too quick—she dodged the bullets without a scratch.

"What *was* that?" the tall thief shouted.

In a flash, Catwoman sprang from behind a display case and kicked the tall thief in the head, sending him sprawling against the short thief. Catwoman scrambled up a post and landed on a display case. The heavyset thief fired at her, but she leaped over the bullet and grabbed a string of white lights hung from the second story molding. Tiny bulbs popped one by one as Catwoman whipped the light string at the thief. Then she dropkicked him.

The tall and short thieves struggled to their feet, but Catwoman sent kick after kick toward them. All three thieves surrounded her, but she wasn't intimidated. Catwoman kicked the tall thief's legs out from under him then delivered a blow to his head. Pouncing, she lifted her hand to scratch his face. The short thief lunged at her from behind, but Catwoman flipped backward, kicking him in the chest and knocking the wind out of him. The heavyset thief stood up, spotting his gun. But Catwoman dove between his legs and reached the gun first. She knocked him out with the butt of the gun.

Catwoman looked down at the three thieves. They hadn't been much trouble. "Mice," she said derisively.

Working quickly, Catwoman gathered the jewels, swept them into the bag, then slipped out the rear door just before the police arrived.

Patience woke up at the foot of her bed, yawned, and stretched. There was a sharp, stabbing pain in her rib, and she reached down to pull a diamond ring from beneath her. She went to put it on her left ring finger, then shook her head.

"Better on the right," she said to herself, admiring the glittering jewel.

Wait a minute, Patience thought after a moment. *Where did that come from?* And then she looked around the room.

Stolen jewels were scattered across the floor. Patience realized that she was still wearing her leather outfit.

I can't believe I did this, Patience thought miserably as she yanked the ring off her finger. *It's wrong. Wrong, wrong, wrong!* Grabbing a paper bag, Patience swept the jewels inside . . . until she came to the claw necklace. She bit her lip. It was so pretty. . . .

Patience stood before her mirror, draping the necklace across her throat. *No,* she thought, *I can't. I won't.*

She dropped the necklace into her drawer—she just couldn't take it back.

A wave of guilt washed over her as she shut the drawer with her hip. But she didn't open it again.

Tom Lone stood beside the jeweler as he flipped through a photo album of stolen items. Lone was the lead detective on the stolen jewelry case, and he was taking notes while the forensics team dusted for fingerprints and searched for fiber and DNA evidence.

"It's one of a kind," the jeweler said, pointing to a photograph of the diamond-tipped

54

claw necklace, "from Egypt. I'm lucky I've got insurance."

"This is some profile," one of the cops, a detective named Swanson, said as he looked over the evidence. "What are we going to call her? Catchick?" he suggested, then thought for a moment. "Catbroad?"

"That seems a little derogatory," one of the other cops piped up.

Swanson frowned. "Whatever, Officer Oprah."

"You two," Lone said, pointing at the cops, "are why I work alone."

"Yo, Tom," one of the investigators called, "check this out." Lone hurried over, and the forensics cop pointed outside the jewelry store's doorway to a white box with a paper bag perched on top of it. Wearing rubber gloves, the forensics cop carefully opened the bag. The stolen jewels glittered inside! And on the bag was one word—SORRY.

The jeweler gasped as he peered over their shoulders. Lone shoved open the door and stepped outside, but there was no one in sight.

Using a pen, the forensics cop lifted the lid of the box slightly. Then he looked up at Lone. "Cupcakes," he explained.

"Please," Patience begged as she stood on the front step of Ophelia Powers's house. "You have to help me. I don't understand what's happening to me." She wasn't sure why, but she felt certain that Ophelia knew the answer and could help her.

But Ophelia didn't respond right away. She simply held the door open wider. Patience stepped inside.

Ophelia led Patience to an enormous two-story library lined with books and ethnic masks. Ophelia walked up the stairs to a shelf and pulled down a thick hardcover. *Bast*, the title read, by Ophelia Powers. Ophelia placed the book on a table and flipped the volume open to a drawing of a beautiful golden cat statue in an ancient Egyptian temple. "The goddess Bast."

Midnight leaped up to the table and stepped

onto the illustration. Patience couldn't help noticing that she bore a strong resemblance to the cat in the drawing as Ophelia moved the cat aside and turned the page. "The Maus are sacred to Bast," Ophelia explained. "They are her messengers."

Patience traced one of the hieroglyphs in the book. "You wrote this?"

"I was a professor for twenty years...until I was denied tenure." Ophelia's lips set in a grim line. "Male academia." She turned to face a sculpture of Bast. "Bast is a rarity," Ophelia went on. "A goddess of the moon and of the sun. She represents the duality in all women. Docile, yet aggressive," Ophelia explained. "Nurturing, yet ferocious."

"So, what..." Patience swallowed hard. For some reason, she didn't want to ask the next question. "What does she have to do with me?"

Ophelia turned her keen eyes on Patience. "What happened the other night?"

"I don't remember," Patience said quickly, backing away toward a balcony.

"Do you want me to tell you?" Ophelia asked.

Patience's heart thudded in her chest. "Yes," she whispered.

Ophelia nodded. "You died," she said simply.

"What?" Patience cried. "I didn't die! I'm right here!" She moved back even further, leaning against a banister.

Ophelia shook her head.

"You're crazy!" Patience shouted. "You're a crazy cat lady!" *It can't be true,* Patience's mind screamed. *It isn't possible!*

Ophelia's grip was gentle but firm as she took Patience by the arms and looked deeply into her eyes. "You died. But . . . you were reborn. Resurrected."

"You're out of your—"

"By the goddess!" Ophelia's voice was a hiss. "By her messenger. By the Mau!"

A feeling of dread came over Patience. Turning, she saw Midnight staring at her with wise golden eyes, and something nudged at the corner of her mind. It was a memory of water, a tidal wave of water rushing at her that night at the Hedare factory. She was drowning. . . .

In the next instant, Ophelia shoved Patience off the balcony.

There was a flash of fear, then Patience twisted in midair and landed on her feet. Snarling, she crouched, ready to attack.

"Midnight saved you," Ophelia called.

A flash tore through Patience's mind—an image of Midnight breathing life into her.

In that moment, the rage seemed to leak from Patience. She crouched on all fours, stunned.

"You're not alone, child," Ophelia said, her voice gentler now. "They've saved others before you. Look." She dropped a stack of papers, which floated down toward Patience like falling snow and scattered on the floor before her. There were a number of different pages—some illustrations, some photos. Patience looked closely at the images as Ophelia stepped down from the balcony to stand beside her.

"You are a catwoman," Ophelia explained. "Every sight, every smell, every sound is incredibly heightened. You possess fierce independence, total confidence, and inhuman reflexes."

Patience heard the words and knew they were true. She stared down at the images. One was a watercolor of an Asian catwoman. Another was of a cat mask. There was even a blurry surveillance photo of a woman in a tight vinyl catsuit. Patience remembered reading about her in the newspaper—Selena Kyle.

Ophelia grabbed a mask from the table behind her. It was beautiful, and almost frightening in its exotic ferocity.

"What do I do now?" Patience asked. "I'm not Patience anym—"

"You *are* Patience," Ophelia snapped, cutting her off. "And you're Catwoman. Duality personified." She held out the beautiful mask. "Accept it, child. You've spent a lifetime caged up. In accepting who you are, *all* of who you are . . . you can be free. . . ."

Patience sat on the floor of her apartment, working feverishly. Now the memories of the night she died were coming quickly, and she felt the urge—no, the need—to put her energy to work. She yanked at the necklace until the claws flew off. Perfect. Next, she used a claw to punch through the fingers of a leather glove.

Her mind reeled as she remembered running through the factory, being chased by Wesley and Armando.

Patience slashed at the ethnic mask with a pair of scissors, modifying the design. She used her new diamond-tipped claw gloves to scratch at her leather pants. The diamond claws tore the toes off her boots as she remembered water, drowning....

Her claws tore through the sleeves of the leather jacket, ripping them free. Catwoman tied her new mask over her face as she looked down at the Hedare logo on her drafting table.

She remembered Midnight breathing into her face. She remembered being left for dead at the Hedare factory.

Catwoman's claws ripped across the Hedare logo.

It was time to get some answers.

Chapter Six

Catwoman scampered across the city rooftops, heading for the Hedare factory. She leaped from building to building, ripped leather pants stretching across her legs, diamond claws extended from her long black gloves. She wore two silver belts crisscrossed over her torso and the black mask she had fashioned from the jersey cloth and ethnic mask—the leather reached down between her eyes and up to two pointed ears.

Catwoman felt her senses prickle. She stopped and cocked her head, then turned her head to see Armando flicking away a cigarette.

Another memory flashed through her mind. Armando had fired a gun at her.

Gritting her teeth, Catwoman narrowed her eyes as Armando stepped into a limousine. The car pulled away, and Catwoman followed, leaping from rooftop to rooftop.

When Armando slipped into a nightclub, Catwoman was right behind him. The dark room throbbed with techno music and strobe lights as Catwoman followed Armando to the bar. Dancers gyrated on elevated stages around the room.

The bartender's eyes went wide at the sight of Catwoman. "What can I do . . . for you?"

"White Russian," Catwoman commanded as she swayed slightly to the music, "no ice, hold the vodka and Kahlua."

The bartender thought for a moment, then turned to fill the order. "Cream, straight up," he said, handing her a shot glass.

Catwoman slugged back the glass of cream, licked her lips, and spotted Armando moving toward the dance floor.

Dancing after him, Catwoman leaped onto a raised platform, where two dancers in black leather moved to the beat. The dancers had a whip. "Gimme," Catwoman purred, snatching the whip. She cracked it a few times, and the crowd dancing below her let out a cheer. Catwoman began to dance, moving to the beat of the music. On all fours, she scratched at a metal pole, then cracked her whip against it. The whip held fast, coiled around the pole, and Catwoman swung around it, then scampered up it to hang upside down. She was next to Armando. Catwoman leaped down and made her way toward him, cracking her whip only inches from his face. Armando started, then grinned as Catwoman playfully wrapped the whip around his throat and pulled him onto the stage.

Armando looked surprised as she led him backstage . . . and shoved him out the rear exit. Flying through the door, Armando fell on his back in the alley.

Catwoman sprang after him, landing on his chest. "Ouch," she growled. "That felt good."

Shoving her away, Armando searched in his coat for his gun.

"You lost," Catwoman purred. "I found." She

pulled out the gun, holding it by the barrel, then tossed it into a nearby trashcan. Armando lunged after it, but Catwoman cracked her whip at his throat. She pulled him close for a second, then gave the whip a yank, sending him spinning across the alley. He slammed into a wall.

"Do you know me?" Catwoman asked as Armando struggled to his feet.

Catwoman kicked him viciously, sending him sprawling face-first to the ground.

"I know *you*," Catwoman snarled. She placed her knee between his shoulders and yanked his head back by the hair.

"What do you want?" Armando shouted.

"The other night, you killed somebody." Catwoman slammed Armando's head against the pavement. "She was—a good person. She was a friend of mine." Slam. "Why did you do it?"

Armando shook his head. He was clearly frightened, but he didn't say anything. Catwoman grabbed Armando's tongue between two of her diamond-tipped claws. "Cat got your tongue?" she demanded, hauling him to his feet by the tongue. "Bet you saw that one coming."

Armando choked as Catwoman slammed him in the gut with her knee. He stumbled backward, falling to the ground as she released him.

"This would be a lot more fun if you'd play along," Catwoman growled at him. "I'm going to ask you nicely one more time." She reached toward him with her claws only inches from his eyes. "Then I'm going to stop acting like a lady."

"I just do what I'm told!" Armando cried in a strangled voice.

"Not for much longer," Catwoman said coldly, inching toward him with her claws.

Reflexively, Armando squeezed shut his eyes. "I don't know your friend! They just told me to flush the pipes. That's all. I didn't know—"

In her mind, Catwoman saw the tidal wave rushing toward her. "Why?" Her voice was a low rumble.

"Maybe she heard something she wasn't supposed to hear!"

"But what?" Catwoman demanded.

"I don't know!" Armando insisted. "Beau-line! There's something wrong with Beau-line!"

Of course, Catwoman thought. *It all makes sense.* "And Hedare is covering it up."

Armando nodded.

"Well, isn't that a kick in the head." With that, Catwoman kicked Armando in the head, knocking him out cold.

She frowned down at him. It was better than he deserved.

Catwoman dropped into the Hedare factory through an open skylight. Moving quickly, she made her way to the door to the research and development department. She hesitated before the door, remembering. This was where she had overheard the information that had gotten her killed.

Catwoman threw open the door, but when she stepped inside, she saw that the place had been ransacked. Papers were scattered everywhere. Shards of glass and plastic lay in piles on the floor where equipment had been smashed and computers overturned.

A memory flashed in her mind: A woman's face on the monitor. Looking younger and younger . . . then decaying.

Catwoman stepped further into the room and spotted someone lying on the floor, unmoving. It was Dr. Slavicky. Someone had shot him in the chest. Catwoman walked toward him and leaned over the body. She knew without touching him that he was dead.

In the distance, sirens began to wail. Catwoman's head jerked up, and her eyes narrowed just as an elderly janitor stumbled into the office. He gaped at her standing over Slavicky, then backed away in fear. "Please . . . don't kill me," he begged.

Catwoman darted past him, through the open door.

Sally was watching the news when Patience came to visit her at the hospital. Patience had brought a small overnight bag full of Sally's things. Patience strode confidently into the room. She felt good. She was wearing stylish new clothes and felt more comfortable in her own skin than she could ever remember feeling before.

Sally's eyes grew wide when she saw Patience. "First: Wow." Sally paused to take in Patience's new haircut and clothes. "You look amazing. Second: This guy is really good for you, obviously. Bet you're glad I pushed you into it. Props to Sally, right?"

Patience smiled. "Props to Sally." Patience put the bag down on the bed. "Are you going to be okay?"

"They still don't know what it is," Sally said as she stirred at her revolting-looking hospital food. "So in the interests of hospital policy, they're releasing me anyway. I do feel better. Maybe I should lay off the chocolate and cosmos more often." Sally pointed to the television set mounted from the ceiling. "Check this out. Some crazy chick in a catsuit murdered Slavicky last night."

Patience felt her stomach grow cold as she looked warily at the screen, which flashed a police sketch of Catwoman.

I don't look like that, Patience thought, staring at the mean-looking woman in the drawing. *Do I?*

"Mark my words," an on-screen image of George Hedare told a group of reporters. "The actions of this lunatic will not keep Beau-line off the shelves. We will launch next week, as scheduled. Because we owe it to the women of this country. Because we owe it to the memory of our fallen colleague."

Patience had to work to steady her breathing. She was furious—Hedare was lying. He was blaming her for a murder he committed.

"What a phony," Sally said absently. She pulled the tiny tub of Beau-line from her bag. "Damn, I'm almost out."

Patience took the bottle from Sally. "Sal, how long have you been having those headaches?"

"A few months."

"Do me a favor: Stop using this."

Sally frowned. "Why?"

Patience looked down at the bottle. "'To Be More,'" she read aloud. It was the Beau-line slogan. Patience tossed the bottle into a trash container marked with the orange biohazard symbol and slammed the lid. "You're enough."

A file dropped onto Lone's desk, but he didn't look up.

"Uh, Tom?" said the detective who had delivered the file. His name was Bob Johnson. "About the Slavicky homicide. Maybe you want to take a look at this?"

"Bob? Would your wife crawl out on the ledge of a building to rescue a stray cat?" Lone asked.

Johnson shrugged. "Maybe if the cat was carrying a pizza."

Lone's lips twisted into a wry smile. "Thanks."

As Johnson walked off, Lone's eye fell on the cardboard coffee cup Patience had given him the other day, the one with the word "Sorry" drawn on it. For some reason, he hadn't been able to throw it away, so he'd placed it in the corner of his desk, next to a basketball trophy and a photo of his parents. A faint smile played on Lone's face, and then he looked down at a plastic evidence bag on his desk. Inside was the paper bag that Catwoman had used to return the stolen jewels. "Sorry," the bag read.

The handwriting was strangely similar....

Feeling uneasy, Lone stood up and walked to the forensics lab. A few moments later, the graphologist had an image of both words projected onto a large white screen.

"Were they written by the same person?" Lone asked, trying to quell the fear in his stomach.

"There *is* a similarity," the graphologist admitted. "The shape of the 'S,' the loop on the 'Y.' But this first one—" He pointed to the coffee cup handwriting. "The broad spacing of the letters is indicative of loneliness. The 'O' means she is reaching out, insecure—the handwriting of a people pleaser. Now, look at the harsh stroke of the 'R' here." The graphologist turned his attention to the writing on the paper bag from the jewelry store. "This woman is very self-confident, almost angry. The 'O'... this one doesn't play by the rules."

Lone breathed a sigh of relief. "So they're different people."

The graphologist shrugged. "Very. It's not an exact science. But put these two women in the same room? It could get interesting." He flipped off the overhead projector and began to gather some papers. "Got a big weekend planned, Tom?"

Lone grinned. "I do now."

"Aren't you supposed to let me win?" Lone asked as the carnival barker handed Patience yet another stuffed animal. Lone had brought her to the community center's benefit fair. It was a fundraiser to help pay for activities for the neighborhood kids, some of whom were waiting nearby, watching Patience with admiration as she won game after game.

Patience smiled at Lone. "I'm not that kind of girl."

"What kind is that?" Lone asked, waggling his eyebrows.

"A loser."

Lone accepted another ball from the carnival barker. "Can I ask you a question?"

"Who did my hair?" Patience joked.

Lone smiled. "I like it." He handed her the ball. "You worked for Hedare. Anybody have a grudge against the company?"

Jolted by the question, Patience chucked the ball at a pyramid of wooden milk bottles, and missed them entirely. "George Hedare isn't the nicest man in the world," she said carefully.

"Somebody was murdered at his factory last night."

Patience's next throw went wild, nearly taking the head off of the carnival barker.

"Sorry!" Patience called to the barker, then turned to Lone. "He has a lot of enemies. He fired me."

"I heard."

Patience looked up at Lone in surprise, then batted her eyelashes playfully. "Am I a suspect, detective?"

It was now Lone's turn. He wound up and

heaved a ball at the pyramid of bottles. They fell over with a satisfying crash.

Lone turned to Patience. "No," he told her gently.

After sampling the games, Patience and Lone climbed aboard the Ferris wheel. The two were squeezed tightly together into the small rattle-trap car. "Look," Lone said as they rose into the air, "you can see all the way... across the street." Suddenly, the wheel gave a creak and a groan, then came to a stop. "Oops," Lone said with a grin. "We might be up here for a while."

Patience snuggled closer to him. "Are you in a hurry?"

Lone turned to look at her, and Patience was suddenly aware of how close their faces were. How close their lips were. Lone leaned forward....

Just then the Ferris wheel gave a sudden, violent lurch. The cars rocked back and forth, almost spinning under the force of the jolt. Patience slammed against Lone as riders and onlookers burst into screams.

Looking down, Lone saw a panicked carnival worker struggling with the emergency brake. But it was no use. From the top of the wheel, Lone could see that a gear had come undone at the center of the machine. It ground against the other gears, jerking the Ferris wheel every time it slipped. Black smoke began to rise from the bowels of the motor.

"Hey!" Lone shouted to the carnie, "The gears!"

But it was no use—the worker couldn't hear him over the noise. Lone could see that the gear could come undone at any moment. If that happened, the entire Ferris wheel would spin out of control.

The Ferris wheel gave a vicious lurch, sending the cars rocking back and forth. Patience grabbed Lone to keep from falling as screams rose around her.

"Hang on!" Lone shouted to Patience. Assessing the situation quickly, Lone carefully climbed out of the car and onto the support bar. He picked his way down toward the gears.

PATIENCE SHARES A LAUGH ON THE BASKETBALL COURT.

TOM LONE, DETECTIVE AND NICE GUY.

PATIENCE AND LONE PLAY SOME ONE-ON-ONE.

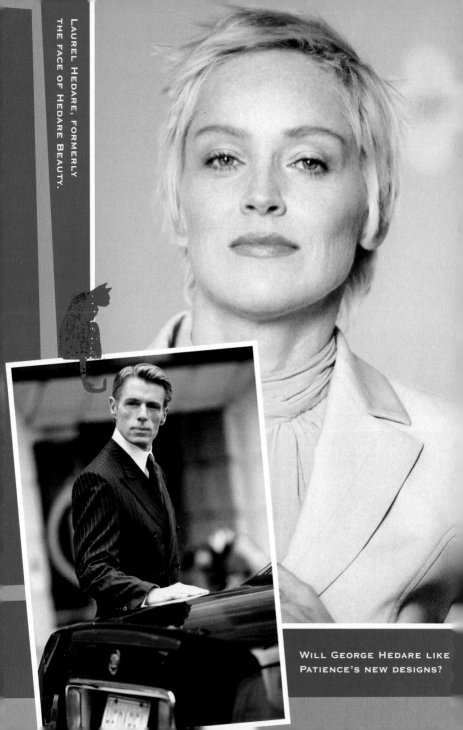

LAUREL HEDARE, FORMERLY THE FACE OF HEDARE BEAUTY.

WILL GEORGE HEDARE LIKE PATIENCE'S NEW DESIGNS?

OH, NO! PATIENCE IS LATE IN DROPPING OFF HER REVISED SKETCHES FOR HER BOSS, GEORGE HEDARE.

PATIENCE IS TIRED OF BEING BULLIED BY HER BOSS. SHE TELLS GEORGE EXACTLY WHAT SHE THINKS OF HIM.

WILL PATIENCE GET OUT
OF THE HEDARE FACTORY ALIVE?

SHAKEN AND DIRTY,
PATIENCE TAKES IN
WHAT HAS HAPPENED.

LONE AND PATIENCE GO FOR A SPIN
ON THE FERRIS WHEEL.

AFTER A FERRIS WHEEL MISHAP, PATIENCE LOWERS
A LITTLE BOY INTO LONE'S ARMS AND TO SAFETY.

LONE INTERROGATES HIS GIRLFRIEND.

PATIENCE USES HER CATLIKE AGILITY TO FIND A SECRET WAY IN.

NOT SO FAST, LAUREL.

Suddenly, a horrifying wail clawed its way through Patience's focus. A small boy, alone in the car across from hers, was crying in terror. His mother was on the ground, screaming.

Patience's breath caught in her throat. "Oh, hang on, boy!" she whispered.

The wheel lurched again, more violently than before, and the little boy let out a shriek as he spilled from his car. He gripped the handrail desperately, his feet dangling in midair.

Reflexively, Patience leaped to the rail above her. With sure-footed grace, she slinked toward the center hub, passing right over Lone, who was nearing the bottom. He didn't look up.

The gears were slamming viciously against each other as Lone reached them. He spotted a small crossbar that had come loose from all of the shaking. Grabbing it, Lone managed to pull it from its mooring. He continued toward the gears, crossbar in hand.

Meanwhile, Patience hurried toward the little boy. His fingers were beginning to slip. *There's no time!* Patience realized, and leaped the last ten feet, landing with one arm wrapped around the boy and the other hand clinging to the back of the seat.

Just then, Lone reached the center of the wheel. Using his legs to hold himself in place, Lone took the crossbar and jammed it between the spinning gears. With a piercing metallic shriek, the gears caught, and the shaking stopped.

The crowd that had gathered below let out a cheer.

"It's okay, baby," Patience said to the little boy in her arm. "Scary ride, huh?"

The boy nodded, sniffling, and Patience gave him a comforting smile. Just then, the boy's seat broke loose, tipping Patience and the boy into midair. For one horrifying second, Patience felt her grip on the boy come loose. Quickly, Patience wrapped her arm around the crossbar and caught the boy with her legs. He clung to them like he would never let go. Patience looked around for the best way down.

"I've got you," said a voice from below.

Patience glanced down, and saw Lone

standing on top of a ticket booth directly below. *Oh, no*, Patience thought, suddenly realizing that she was in full Catwoman mode, *what am I doing? I'm going to completely blow my cover!* She forced herself to look grateful and relieved, instead of grim and determined.

"Easy," Lone coached the carnies as they manipulated the Ferris wheel gears by hand. "Little more..."

The wheel turned slowly, lowering Patience and the boy toward Lone. Lone reached out for the little boy. "I've got you," he said.

The boy hesitated, looking up at Patience. He clearly didn't want to let go of her, but Patience gave him a nod, and he fell into Lone's arms.

Below, the crowd that had gathered around the Ferris wheel let out an enormous cheer. Patience looked down at Lone, who was still holding the boy. "Thank you," she mouthed.

A few moments later, Patience found herself back on the ground, watching as the little boy hugged his crying mother. Patience turned to Lone, who was staring up at the Ferris wheel— at the car they started out in and the car she ended up in. He couldn't quite figure out how she could have gotten over there . . . unless she flew. "I'm not sure how you did it." Lone said slowly." But I'm impressed."

"I saw how you did it," Patience replied, wrapping him in her arms, ". . . and so am I."

Chapter Seven

"We should celebrate," Lone said as he and Patience walked across the fair grounds. "How about dinner? Unless..."

"I'd love to," Patience said quickly. "I want to. But I can't, not tonight." Patience wanted to go, but Catwoman already had a date . . . with George Hedare.

Lone was clearly disappointed, but he tried to recover. "Oh," he said. "Well, I shouldn't, either. Crimes are being committed as we speak. I should go make the city a safer place."

Patience smiled. "That sounds like a nice way to spend an evening," she said, almost to herself.

Lone was definitely her kind of guy.

Catwoman looked up at the security camera mounted atop a ten-foot gate adorned with an ironwork H. The Hedare mansion. *Very nice*, Catwoman thought as she flicked her whip at the camera, knocking it in another direction. Then she leaped to the top of the wall, landing in a crouch, and scrambled up a trellis to a second-story window. The room was dark, but it was definitely what she was looking for—shelves lined with leather-bound books, a large desk—George Hedare's study. She jumped to the ledge and peered in. With one diamond-tipped claw, Catwoman carved a circle in the glass. Knocking the glass piece into the room, she unlatched the window and swung herself inside.

Catwoman strode to the desk and began flipping through computer disks. There was nothing on Beau-line. She strode into the hall.

Wham!

Feeling a sharp pain in the back of her head, Catwoman fell and rolled down the stairs. She stood up just as someone flipped on the lights.

It was Laurel Hedare, dressed in silk pajamas, wielding a golf club. *That's an interesting golfing look*, Catwoman thought as Laurel made her way down the stairs to where Catwoman lay on the landing.

"You picked the wrong house to rob," Laurel snarled.

Laurel nudged Catwoman with her foot. Then, seemingly satisfied that Catwoman was knocked out cold, she leaned forward—

Catwoman sprang up and grabbed the golf club. Laurel backed away as Catwoman tossed the club across the room.

"You're that cat," Laurel said, suddenly wary. "The one who killed Slavicky."

"Now, Laurel," Catwoman growled, "You shouldn't believe everything you see on TV."

"What do you want?" Laurel demanded.

"Is the 'man of the house' at home?"

"Why on earth would he be home?" Laurel snapped. "*I'm* here."

"It's too bad he missed me," Catwoman said. "I hear he loves cats."

Darting suddenly, Laurel tried to break past

Catwoman toward the stairs. But Catwoman pounced and the two tumbled down the steps together.

"If you've got a problem with him, maybe we can work it out," Laurel suggested as Catwoman leaned against her chest. "Girl to girl?"

"Oh, that'd be fun!" Catwoman purred sarcastically. "We could make s'mores and do each other's hair and talk about boys."

Laurel arched her back, throwing Catwoman off balance. Laurel scrambled away and jumped to her feet.

"If your husband ever comes home again," Catwoman said, unperturbed, "tell him I know all about Beau-line."

Laurel stopped cold and stared at Catwoman. "What about Beau-line?"

"It's disease in a jar," Catwoman spat. "I wouldn't caulk a sink with it."

"Nonsense," Laurel replied. "I've been using it for years."

"It's your funeral." Catwoman said, preening her claws. "Because whoever killed Slavicky did it to keep Beau-line's toxic little secret. And Slavicky wasn't the first."

Laurel backed away. "You're suggesting that my husband . . . is a murderer?"

"I'm suggesting," Catwoman clarified, "that you tell me where he is, so I can ask him myself."

Laurel's eyes were wide as she digested the information. "I guess . . ." she said slowly, "I should be shocked. I should protest his innocence and tell you he would never do such things. . . ."

Catwoman felt a trace of pity for Laurel. It wasn't her fault that her husband was a killer. And she was a victim of Beau-line, too. Laurel stared at Catwoman a moment, then moved to a table. She moved a cell phone aside to rummage through some mail. "The truth is, that man is capable of anything," Laurel finished. After a moment, she pulled out a glossy invitation and held it up. HYDROPOLIS, the invitation read. Underneath was an address. "This is where you can find George," Laurel said.

Catwoman took the invitation. "Thanks."

"If what you said about Beau-line is true, I won't be party to it," Laurel said decisively. "I want to help. How can I reach you?"

Thinking for a moment, Catwoman grabbed the cell phone on the table and held it up. "I'm not listed. I'll take yours." She strode to the door, then turned back for a moment. After all, Laurel had been kind to Patience. This situation wasn't her fault. "For what it's worth, I'm sorry."

Laurel shook her head slightly. "I built my life around him."

Catwoman nodded sympathetically. "It's time to get your own."

By the time Catwoman arrived at the theatre, the place was already crowded with spectators, paparazzi, and security. Catwoman stalked around the building, finally spotting a large glass façade. She scaled it quickly, then leaped from the top to a second-story balcony. Finding an unlocked door, Catwoman slipped inside.

Onstage, acrobats and dancers in vibrant colors performed on trapezes, tightropes, and bungee cords. Their costumes were done in green and blue silk, and flowed in the breeze created by an enormous fan.

But Catwoman wasn't paying attention to the show. She spotted Hedare sitting in a box directly opposite—sitting with the new Hedare model, Drina. Catwoman smiled as Drina got up and stepped out of the box, apparently in a huff.

"I love this part," Catwoman hissed as she slipped lightly into the chair beside Hedare.

Hedare gave a start. "What the—"

"Like my nails? I just had them done."

Catwoman slashed him across the cheek just as the music reached its peak, drowning out Hedare's anguished cry. Hedare lunged toward the exit, but Catwoman was too quick. Shoving a chair against the door, she advanced on him. Blood dripped from the cuts on Hedare's face, staining his white tuxedo shirt.

"Ooh, my bad," Catwoman purred. "You can take the cat out of the alley, but you just can't take the alley out of the cat." She grabbed Hedare.

"Get your paws off me this instant," Hedare barked.

Catwoman slammed him against the wall and wrapped a hand around his throat, so that the diamond tips of her claws dug into his skin.

"I know all about Beau-line," Catwoman said as she tightened her grip. "I know it's poison, and I know you're covering it up." She didn't even look up as the door began to rattle with the force of people trying to get in. "So you killed my girl Patience," Catwoman went on. "You killed her because of Beau-line."

"What?" Hedare demanded, his eyes bulging. "I fired her."

When will you rodents learn that lying only makes it worse? Catwoman wondered, gritting her teeth. "Sad, isn't it? That your last words will be a lie. Oh, well."

Just then, the door to the box flew open and uniformed cops flooded in, guns drawn. Hissing in frustration, Catwoman flung Hedare to the side and leaped to the lip of the box.

But the aisles below were swarming with police officers.

In a flash, Catwoman leaped toward the stage and grabbed a trapeze. Performers scattered around her as she swung toward an acrobat on a bungee cord, landed on his back, and hurled herself into the rafters.

The audience let out a cheer, thinking Catwoman's performance was part of the show.

Catwoman leaped between ropes, slashing them with her claws as she passed. The cops below scattered as sandbags crashed to the floor and exploded.

She had almost reached the light grid when a voice shouted, "Hold it right there!"

Tom Lone was climbing a ladder toward the grid, his gun trained on Catwoman.

"Cats come when we feel like it," Catwoman said casually, "not when we're told."

Reaching the grid, Lone picked his way toward Catwoman. It was dark above the lights, but Catwoman could still make out his intense eyes.

He stepped forward, but the flimsy support gave way under his feet. Lone lost his balance—

Catwoman sprang forward, grabbing his

gun arm. She looked at him a moment, then snatched the gun from his hand and tossed it aside. Catwoman yanked Lone toward her and licked his cheek.

"You're under arrest," Lone said, but it was too late.

Catwoman bounded away easily, stalking the narrow railings.

Lone went after her, moving more slowly and carefully.

Catwoman reached the end of the railings and found herself trapped. There was nothing but a mesh platform and a twenty-five-foot drop to the floor below.

"Now we're playing," Catwoman said as Lone advanced on her.

"You're playing," he corrected. "I'm at work."

Catwoman's eyes narrowed. "And something tells me right now you love your job."

Advancing on her, Lone pulled out his handcuffs.

"What," Catwoman asked in a sultry voice, "You're going to arrest me?"

Lone lunged toward her, but Catwoman

dodged and kicked his leg out from under him. Falling, Lone almost dropped the cuffs, but he recovered and landed a mean kick to Catwoman's stomach.

He advanced on her again, but Catwoman gave a fearsome jump, grabbing an overhead electrical cable and swinging away. Lone let out a cry as he pitched forward, losing his balance. Like a pendulum, Catwoman swung back and wrapped her legs under his arms and around his chest, saving him from falling once again. Once they were both over the platform, Catwoman tried to kick him off, but Lone grabbed her legs and gave a fierce heave, snapping the cable.

Suddenly, the stage was plunged into darkness. Sparks flew as Lone and Catwoman plummeted to the platform. Catwoman grabbed the cable just before it struck the mesh.

"Careful!" Lone shouted. "If that thing hits us, we're both fried!"

Catwoman leaned close. "I knew I felt a spark between us," she whispered. Turning, she flung the cable away just as Lone reached for her mask.

"Please—" she snarled, slapping his hand,

"it's our first date." Her face was close to his.

"Don't flatter yourself, lady," Lone replied. "I'm taken." He struggled to free himself, but Catwoman kept her legs wrapped around him in a viselike grip.

Catwoman leaned toward him. "Really?" she taunted. "Does she know about . . . us?"

"There's no us," Lone snapped. "Just a cop and a cat he's going to collar." He twisted himself out of her thigh lock and rolled on top of her.

"Is your girl *purr*-fect?" Catwoman asked playfully. "Like me?"

"She's not like you at all."

Lone and Catwoman were face-to-face. She grinned at him and purred.

Quickly, Lone got to his feet. He had snapped a handcuff on her, finally. "It's over," Lone announced. He gave the cuff a yank . . . but it came up empty.

Catwoman had slithered out of the handcuff. She sprang to her feet, laughing.

She looked over at the grid, where more cops were advancing on them. Others covered the exits, below. Thinking he had her cornered, Lone

stepped up behind Catwoman—

She leaped, grabbing the dangling power line. It tore from the ceiling, and Catwoman dropped with it to the floor. A group of cops advanced on her, guns drawn, and she backed toward the wall. Looking over, Catwoman spotted a circuit breaker panel. *Just a whisker away*, she thought.

"Show of hands—" Catwoman called to the cops. "Who can see in the dark?" Catwoman lifted a dainty hand, then slammed the power cable into the circuit breakers.

Bang!

There was a flash, then a waterfall of sparks as the theater was plunged into darkness. There were screams from the audience as the patrons panicked. No one could see a thing.

Except Catwoman.

"This is a disaster!" Hedare bawled into the phone as he searched through file boxes in his study. "A total disaster!" He winced. The slashes on his cheek burned painfully beneath white bandages whenever he spoke. "How does she know all this, anyway? Who is she and what—" Hedare's voice died in his throat as he looked up to see Laurel standing in the doorway. Hedare narrowed his eyes and slammed the phone back into its receiver.

"It's all right, darling," Laurel said calmly. "Don't be scared."

"You have no idea," Hedare bellowed. "We are on the brink of ruin! And your brilliant advice to me is 'Don't be scared'?"

Laurel's eyes glittered like ice. "No," she said slowly, sauntering toward him. "My advice to you is: Quit the self-tanning, resist the urge to date children born on the same day cell phones were invented, and for God's sake, George," she added through gritted teeth, "just once in your miserable life *be...a...man*."

Hedare slapped Laurel, hard. Shooting pain ran up his arm, and Hedare cried out in agony. It was as though he had just slapped a marble statue. He stared at his wife. Laurel hadn't flinched.

And her expression was as hard as her face.

Chapter Eight

Patience stood in the middle of her apartment, holding up two outfits. One was very demure, the other very daring. "Which one?" Patience asked.

Sally shook her head. "I don't know. Do you want him to take you to church or the Playboy mansion?"

Patience threw both outfits aside in frustration. "It's just . . ." She sighed. "I am just a mess right now."

"Look, I can be a mess, too, like Thursday through Sunday," Sally confessed. "Big deal."

Patience gave her friend a wry smile. *Somehow, I think my being a mess is on a slightly bigger scale*, she thought. "But what if he doesn't like—"

"He can't pick and choose, Patience," Sally said, interrupting gently. "If he wants it to work, he has to like all of you. Love the girl, love her problems, right?"

Patience heaved a sigh. If Sally only knew...

Patience sat in the booth at the Japanese restaurant, her face pressed against the glass of an aquarium. A kaleidoscope of colorful tropical fish swam idly inside. Patience licked her lips.

"Pretty," said a voice behind Patience.

She turned and saw Lone standing behind her. Blushing, Patience stepped out of the booth and straightened her clothes. In the end, Sally had taken her shopping. They'd ended up with something that straddled the line between demure and sexy. Patience was glad that Lone seemed to like it. "Thank you," she said.

"You, too," Lone said, smiling. "But I meant the fish."

They took their seats and placed their order. Patience found herself staring at the lantern above the table. Its fringe was distracting her, swaying temptingly just beyond her reach.

"Paperwork," Lone said as he poured them each a glass of sake.

Patience forced herself to tune into the conversation. Lone had been saying something about why he was late.

"There was a mountain of it," he went on. "There's enough when you catch them, but when you don't..."

Patience tore her eyes away from the fringe. "Tell me about the one that got away."

Lone looked away for a moment, and Patience took the opportunity to swat at the lamp. She just couldn't help herself. *No more*, she commanded herself, lowering her hand.

When Lone turned back, he stared at the swinging lamp for a moment.

"Catwoman," Lone said thoughtfully, still gazing at the lamp. "Have you heard of her?"

Patience nodded, barely trusting herself to speak. But Lone seemed to expect her to say something. "Yeah," she said finally. "She carries a whip."

Lone shook his head and shifted in his seat

uncomfortably. "She kissed me."

"Really." Patience did her best to keep her voice neutral, but there was something exciting in hearing Lone confide in her about herself. And there was something else. *Can I be feeling jealous?* Patience wondered. *Is that even possible?*

Lone chuckled. "Yeah," he admitted. "What do you think of that?"

Just then, a waiter arrived, placing an enormous tray of sushi between them. Patience eyed the tray hungrily—those tropical fish had made her ravenous. "That depends," she told Lone, smiling. "Do you like bad girls?" She peeled a piece of fish off of its bed of rice and popped it into her mouth, licking her fingers.

"Only if they like me back," Lone joked. He poured a measured amount of soy sauce into a small rectangular dish and began to mix in some wasabi. "I'm a cop, Patience," he said suddenly. " 'Bad' isn't something that tempts me. It's something I lock up."

Patience swallowed her fish and shrugged. "Come on," she replied. "Good, bad. There's got to be a place in between. It might be a little more complicated than you think."

Lone looked at her for a moment. "How about we start talking about you?" Lone suggested, shifting gears. "What's it like to be an artist?"

"I'm not really an artist," Patience confessed. "I mean, I went to art school. Drawing was really the only thing I was good at. Then I got a regular job in advertising." Patience heaved a heavy sigh. "Now I don't know what I am anymore." *In more ways than one*, she added mentally.

"You're different," Lone told her gently, his dark eyes full of sincerity. "You're special."

Patience's heart gave an involuntary flutter. "Thanks," she said, remembering how Lone had told Catwoman the night before that he was taken.

"It's true," Lone added warmly. "And I want to know more about you."

"You want to know more?" Patience's eyebrows flew up.

"Definitely," Lone said.

Lone gazed down at Patience as she stirred and stretched in her sleep. She looked beautiful, dozing on the couch. Trying not to wake her, Lone crossed the room. He drank a glass of water in the bathroom, then headed back toward Patience.

Sharp pain tore through the bottom of his foot. Cursing softly, Lone lifted his bare foot and pulled out something strange. It almost looked like a diamond-tipped claw. Lone studied it for a moment before the truth sank in. The cup and the bag that were both marked with "Sorry." The way Patience had saved that boy in the Ferris wheel. Everything started to make sense. Lowering himself shakily into a chair, Lone looked back at Patience's sleeping form. She didn't look dangerous now....

Toying lightly with the glass in his hand, Lone wondered how he could prove his hunch that Patience and Catwoman were the same person. Absently, he glanced down at the glass he used for his water. There was a lipstick mark on the rim. And the lab had collected a sample of the lipstick Catwoman had left on his cheek the night before....

Patience woke to the electronic chirp of a cell phone. "Tom?" she called, still half-asleep. No answer.

The phone continued its song. Patience reached down and pulled the cell phone Laurel gave her out of the pocket of her leather pants. "Hello?"

"It's me," Laurel's voice said at the other end of the line. "You were right. I can't believe it, but you were right."

Patience was distracted, still looking for signs of Lone. *He must have gone home after I nodded off,* she thought.

"I've got proof," Laurel went on. "We have to stop him. We can stop him *together*."

There was a note on the chair. Patience scanned it. "Something came up," the note read, "T." Patience frowned. *That's pretty cold,* she thought, anger sending a dagger through her heart. She turned her full attention to the voice on the cell phone.

"George is launching Beau-line at a press conference tomorrow." Laurel's voice sounded panicked. "It'll be on the shelves by Monday."

Patience crumpled the note. Now all of her attention was turned on the phone in her hand. "Where are you?" she growled.

Catwoman had no trouble leaping from a tree onto the sill at the Hedare mansion, then pulling herself into the sunroom. Landing lightly on her feet, she straightened and looked around the room.

"Thank goodness you came." Laurel's voice sounded relieved as she appeared in the doorway.

"What did you find?"

"Enough evidence to put someone away for a long, long time," Laurel said conspiratorially. She turned, and Catwoman followed her through the sunroom.

"This can't be easy for you," Catwoman said sympathetically.

"I was everything they wanted me to be," Laurel said, almost to herself. "I was never more beautiful. I was never more powerful. Then I turned forty . . . and they threw me away."

Quietly, the two women entered George's study.

"It's all there," Laurel said, nodding. "Behind the desk."

Catwoman stepped behind the massive oak desk, and saw George Hedare's body sprawled on the floor. Bullets had ripped through his chest, and there were ugly claw marks all over his body. He wasn't moving.

"How'd I do?" Laurel asked playfully. "The clawed flesh thing was a little tricky, but I think I pulled it off."

Catwoman gaped at Laurel. "You killed him."

Laurel's expression hardened. "No one's going to stop Beau-line from hitting the shelves," she said. "Not Slavicky, not George. And especially not you. But forgive me. I'm being rude." She took something from the table. Catwoman couldn't quite make out what the thing was—it was wrapped in a handkerchief. "Can I get you anything?" Laurel asked condescendingly.

"Can of tuna?" she suggested. "Saucer of milk?" Just then, she tossed the dark object to Catwoman, who snatched it out of the air.

Catwoman looked down at the thing in her hand. It was a gun. Laurel was still holding the handkerchief.

Laurel grinned. "Smoking gun?"

Catwoman's eyes narrowed as Laurel held up a security alarm remote and pressed a button. The mansion echoed with the scream of an alarm. "Oh, no!" Laurel screamed. "George! George!"

Tensing, Catwoman backed toward the window just as security guards arrived below. Armando stepped up beside them.

"It's the Catwoman! She's got a gun!"

A gun. Realizing her luck, Catwoman lifted the gun and took aim at Laurel.

"It isn't loaded, sweetheart," Laurel said coolly. "You just emptied it into my husband's chest."

Letting out a yowl, Catwoman bounded past Laurel and out the door.

Grinning victoriously, Laurel let her go.

Blue-and-red lights flashed through the windows as Catwoman glanced desperately around the hallway above the foyer. The front door exploded open, and security men rained into the front hall.

Catwoman ran blindly, desperate to find an exit. After a moment, she found herself in Laurel's dressing room. Catwoman scanned the room, trying to find a way out. Suddenly, her eyes froze on a rack of clothes. That gave her an idea. Grabbing a tracksuit, Catwoman shoved the clothes into a canvas laundry bag, then tucked the bag into her belt. She looked out the window and saw cops and security cars swarming the grounds, moving in to surround the building.

Looking down, Catwoman saw paramedics returning an empty gurney to the ambulance. *I guess Hedare was beyond medical help*, Catwoman thought as she climbed out the window. It was the first time she had ever felt sorry for George Hedare.

The paramedics shut the ambulance door and climbed into the cab. The moment the ambulance started to move, Catwoman leaped, landing silently on the roof. When the ambulance drove beneath an overpass, Catwoman scrambled to the underbelly of the freeway, then climbed down to street level and began to yank on the clothes she had stolen from the Hedare mansion.

How could I have been so stupid? Patience thought as she looked over her shoulder, distracted by a screaming siren. *Why did I ever trust Laurel Hedare?* Patience's heart beat like a drum as she wandered through the commercial district, dodging cop cars as they drove past. Suddenly, Patience caught sight of a giant screen. A news broadcast was reporting on Hedare's murder. "Catwoman Kills Again," the headline read. Patience gritted her teeth—she was out of options.

Catwoman had to disappear.

Chapter Nine

"Patience," Lone said the moment she stepped into her apartment. His eyes were clouded, as though hidden in shadow, as he stood in her living room. He was pointing a gun at her. "I . . . I'm sorry."

Blue lights began to flicker through Patience's apartment, leaking in through the window. Lone gazed at her sadly. Looking down at his gun, he added, "I guess you could take this right out of my hands if you wanted."

"If I wanted." Patience's voice was quiet.

Lone put the gun in its holster and pulled out a pair of handcuffs. Patience dropped her head, shoulders slumped, and turned her back to him.

Lone slipped the cuffs over her wrists reluctantly. Then he led her away.

This room lacks a certain charm, Patience thought as she looked around the small, sterile chamber. The room had no windows—just a one-way mirror along the wall. She sat at the table, trying not to let Lone's tense pacing bother her.

"I'm telling you," Patience insisted for what seemed like the thousandth time, "Slavicky had evidence that proved Beau-line was toxic. That's why Laurel killed him! George found out, and she killed him, too. She was covering it up!" *I know this doesn't sound believable at all, even to me*, Patience thought. But it was the truth.

"Ballistics show the same weapon killed both men," Lone stated. "The gun that was in your hand—"

"Catwoman's hand," Patience corrected.

"What's the difference?"

"Does it matter?" Patience asked, her voice

hard as iron. "You think we're both guilty."

Lone rubbed his eyes. They had been over this before. "Don't you understand?" he asked. "All the evidence, every piece, it all points to you. There's nothing that shows me anything different."

"Just me," Patience said quietly. "You could trust me." She looked up into his eyes, but they were like shuttered windows. Patience felt a tear snake down her face, tracing a spidery path down her cheek. She wiped it away. "Do you remember the first time you saw me?"

"Yeah." Lone's voice was thoughtful.

Patience lifted her eyes to meet Lone's. "What did you see?"

"A girl," Lone replied. "Rescuing a cat." The words were hard to get out—he felt as though a claw was tearing at his heart.

Patience shook her head. "No," she said, "you didn't. You saw a crazy person about to jump off a ledge. *All the evidence pointed to that.*" She leaned toward him. "I need you to believe me, Tom."

Lone felt his breath catch in his throat. He

didn't know what to say. He wanted to believe her—he wanted it more than anything in the world. But it just didn't make sense. "How can I?" he asked. "I don't know what you are."

Patience felt as though she had been punched in the stomach. The air left her lungs—she couldn't breathe. "I'm the same girl you went out on a date with last night," she said in a quiet voice.

There seemed to be nothing left to say. Lone crossed to the door and knocked. A cop unlocked it, letting him out. "Take her back," Lone told the cop.

When he left, Patience was completely alone.

Tears still streamed down Patience's face as the jail guard led her toward her holding cell. But with every step, Patience felt her sadness and fear turn to a cold, hard anger. Her eyes flashed dangerously as the guard shoved her into her cell.

"You be a good kitty, now," the guard said, grinning.

Patience's fingers wrapped dangerously around the bars of her cell, and she let out a violent hiss.

Wisely, the guard backed away.

Applause swelled as Laurel Hedare, dressed in black, stepped to the podium. A throng of reporters was clustered before her, desperate to capture every word of the grieving Hedare widow. "My husband dreamed of a world in which every woman was as beautiful as she wanted to be," she said to the crowd in her silken voice. "He dedicated his life to the pursuit of that dream. As Hedare's new chief executive, I intend to make that dream a reality by pro-ceeding with tomorrow's launch of Beau-line."

Flashbulbs went off like a hail of sparks as hands flew up with questions. Laurel grinned.

Nothing could stop her now.

Catwoman was on her haunches in the corner of her cell, unmoving, her hands wrapped tightly around her knees as shouts from prisoners echoed through the jail.

"Lights out," the guard said, and suddenly the room went dark. The moon shone pale and cold onto the floor of Patience's prison cell.

A shadow moved across the window. Patience didn't need to look up to know who it was.

"Hello, Midnight," Patience said, slowly raising her head. Moonlight gleamed across her eyes, making them look hard as obsidian.

Midnight squeezed through the window bars and dropped lightly into the cell. Leaning forward, Patience let her hands drop to the floor in front of her. She tipped toward the ground until she was nose-to-nose with Midnight.

"I love you, baby," Catwoman purred, "but Lassie would have brought me a key." Reaching out, Patience stroked the Mau's fur idly, staring up at the bars the cat had just walked through. Suddenly, Patience's hand froze. Her head cocked, and she turned to look at the larger bars to her cell.

"I take it back," she said suddenly. Rising,

Patience stretched, catlike, and swayed toward the bars. "I accept," Patience announced, rubbing against them.

Licking her hand, Patience guided her arm between the bars. She arched her back and turned her head at an impossible angle, sliding it through. Like a snake, she slithered slowly between the iron bars. She left the bars behind as though she were a phantom.

Once on the other side, Patience stretched and threw a glance at Midnight. "The funny thing about cages," Catwoman remarked. "Is that sometimes the hardest part about getting out is making the decision to leave."

Footsteps echoed down the hall—a guard on his rounds.

Catwoman leaped away.

Finding a window, Patience slid it open and looked out. It was a ten-story drop to the street below. Suddenly, Patience spied a car—a Jaguar—skimming down the road. Patience smiled.

This is the fun part, she thought as she leaped out the window, plunging toward the street below. For a moment, panic gripped her, but Patience forced herself to let go of her fear, and trust in her feline instincts. Her body twisted in midair, and she landed on the pavement on all fours.

There was a hideous squeal of brakes as the Jaguar came to a stop inches behind her.

"Hey!" the driver shouted, leaping from the elegant car. "Are you okay?"

"A girl's got to know how to land on her feet," Patience said calmly as she rose. Before the driver had a chance to react, Patience jumped behind the wheel and took off.

Catwoman was back in action.

"I've been dying to get my hands on this stuff," the female reporter said as she accepted a sample jar of Beau-line from Laurel. Around her, several other reporters had already opened their samples and were busily slathering the beauty cream on their skin.

Laurel smiled graciously. After all, she could afford to be generous. The more people who tried Beau-line, the more who would become hopelessly addicted to it. "Well, my husband would have wanted you all to have it," Laurel said. "He wanted it for everyone."

The reporter stepped away, and a handsome man with intense dark eyes stepped forward.

"Detective Lone?" Laurel forced herself to smile, but she was uneasy at the sight of the policeman. She wanted people to focus on Beau-line, not on her husband's murder. "What a surprise." Fixing upon a way to turn his presence to her advantage, Laurel turned to face the reporters. "I'd like you to meet the man responsible for bringing my husband's killer to justice."

Flashbulbs went off as reporters captured the moment. Lone shifted uneasily on his feet—he never liked being the center of attention. "Mrs. Hedare," he said uncomfortably, "I was wondering if I could have a word with you."

Almost imperceptibly, Laurel's expression flickered. But in an instant, the flash of unease was gone. "Well, ladies and gentlemen," she told the reporters smoothly, "I think we were just about finished. If you'll excuse me."

Laurel led Lone toward the door, but she made sure to give her henchman Wesley a nod first. As usual, the detective didn't have backup—but Laurel never went into a fight without the odds stacked in her favor.

"I saw her standing over him," Laurel said as she leaned against the desk in George Hedare's office. That is, in what used to be George's office. Laurel had already had it completely redecorated and moved in. "There were claw marks all over his body."

Lone frowned at his notebook. "But none on Slavicky's."

Laurel gave a nonchalant shrug. "She didn't have time."

"She also didn't have a motive," Lone pointed out. *I need you to believe me, Tom.* Patience's words echoed in his mind. He looked at Laurel. There was something about her that he didn't trust, and something about Patience that he did. Maybe the evidence *did* suggest that Patience was Catwoman, and that Catwoman had committed the murders. But the evidence didn't explain everything. Tom decided to test his hunch. "What if I told you I know the truth?" he demanded. "That I know who really killed your husband?" Laurel's face didn't change, so Lone decided to play his final card. "That I know about Beau-line...."

"Why, detective," Laurel said coolly, "you make it sound like I'm a suspect."

"What if I told you I had evidence?" Lone asked. This was it—if Laurel didn't take the bait, Lone couldn't test his theory any further. For the first time in his life, Lone found himself praying for someone to be guilty.

Turning back toward her desk, Laurel asked, "If you have evidence, how come I'm not in cuffs?"

Lone noticed that she didn't insist that he couldn't possibly have evidence. He nearly held his breath as he said, "You're a smart woman, Laurel. Beautiful..." His voice took on a deeper timbre as he added, "*Rich*. I thought maybe we could work something out."

Laurel's eyebrow lifted slightly. "It seems you have me over a barrel," she said, her voice cold as ice. She paused a moment, then asked, "This evidence, you'll make it disappear? You'll pin everything on the girl?"

Lone's heart was pounding. "If that's what you want."

"And you?" Laurel asked, her eyes glittering. "How much do you want?"

"You just gave me what I want," Lone said, his voice hardening. "You just told me it was you."

Laurel's eyes narrowed as she took in the situation. "How could you believe I did it?" she asked as she stepped from behind her desk.

"How?" An image of Patience flashed through Lone's mind, and he wondered how he ever could have doubted her. "I finally trusted a friend."

"Well," Laurel snapped, "your friend just got you killed." She lifted her arm. In her hand was a gun.

Lone reached for his sidearm, but Laurel was too quick.

Bam!

Pain screamed through Lone's shoulder as the bullet ripped through his flesh. Staggering back against the wall, Lone dropped his gun.

Laurel closed in on him, kicking his gun away.

"Don't be stupid, Laurel," Lone warned, eyeing the gun in her hand. "You don't want to kill a cop."

"I'm a woman, Lone," Laurel shot back. "I'm used to doing things I don't want to do."

As Laurel raised her pistol, Lone swung desperately at her with his good hand. His fist met her marble face and glanced off, sending agony through his hand.

"What *are* you?" Lone cried.

Laurel gave him a backhanded slap, sending him reeling onto the floor. Her fist was like solid iron.

"I'm more," Laurel said, quoting the Beau-line slogan and aiming the gun at his head.

Lone squeezed shut his eyes.

There was a hiss, and then a crack as a bull-whip snapped around Laurel's gun hand.

The gun flew from Laurel's hand as Catwoman gave the whip a yank and strutted into the room.

"You really thought I was going to let you kill again?" Catwoman demanded. "Think again." Catwoman gave her whip a decisive crack.

Laurel backed away . . . in the direction of Lone's gun. Catwoman rushed to help Lone, never noticing the pistol near Laurel's feet.

"Forget about me," Lone grunted as Catwoman tried to help him to his feet.

"I can't," she admitted. Catwoman managed to haul Lone up and rush him out the door.

"How sweet," Laurel said once she was left alone in her office. "But trust me, it won't end well." She walked back toward her desk. "Thanks," she muttered to herself. "Now I can kill you both." Laurel grabbed the phone and punched in a number. "Get up here," she barked into the receiver. "Now."

It was time for Plan B.

Chapter Ten

Catwoman helped Lone down the corridor and down the stairs. She knew that they had to get out of there right away. Laurel wasn't about to let them get away that easily.

At that moment, Armando came charging up the stairwell, his gun drawn.

Bang!

Catwoman and Lone hurried back up the steps. Reaching out, Catwoman tried a stairwell door. Locked. She cursed under her breath as she and Lone headed farther up. They had to keep climbing until they could get out.

Below them, Laurel joined Armando in the hunt.

Redoubling their speed, Catwoman and Lone

finally reached the last door. Catwoman breathed a sigh of relief as it gave way. As she stepped into the dark room, she felt cool air against her face. It was a large space—a creepy storage room lit only by the moonlight streaming through a wall of windows at the rear. Images of Laurel Hedare were everywhere. All of the old Hedare advertising materials—billboard panels, life-sized posters, and cardboard cutouts—had found their way into this space.

Lone and Catwoman wasted no time. They ducked into the maze of Laurel's past glory.

Armando and Laurel burst into the room, and Wesley arrived by elevator moments later.

"I feel like we're surrounded," Lone whispered as he eyed a series of panels that had once made up a long billboard. Laurel's face was broken into eerie sections—as though she had been cut into strips and pieces.

"That's okay," Catwoman purred. "I didn't come here to run."

Feeling lightheaded, Lone slumped against a billboard, leaving a trail of blood where his shoulder hit the panel. Catwoman steadied him, then guided him into the darkness behind a panel. Lone sank to the floor. He had lost a lot of blood—he didn't have any strength left.

"Listen," Lone said, struggling with his voice, "I want to you to know...I'm sorry. I should have trusted you all along."

A smile played at the corners of Catwoman's mouth. "I think you have me confused with someone else."

"Come on, Patience," Lone said, reaching for her mask.

Catwoman caught him by the wrist, then moved in so that her face was only millimeters from his. "This Patience is a lucky girl." She pulled away. "Stay here," she commanded. "I'll be back when it's safe."

Lone fixed her with his dark eyes. "Why did you come here tonight?" he asked. "To stop her ...or for revenge?"

Catwoman cocked her head. *Isn't the answer obvious?* she wondered. "I came for both."

Turning, Catwoman disappeared into the darkness.

From her perch high atop a billboard featuring Laurel's image, Catwoman watched Armando, Laurel, and Wesley split up. *Like rats in a maze*, Catwoman thought as she crept along the top of the billboard, tracking their progress.

She decided to take on Wesley first.

Wesley noticed a dark shadow fall across his line of vision. He looked up—just in time to see Catwoman leaping down on him.

In a single, fluid move, Catwoman caught his gun hand and rolled, flipping Wesley onto the floor. She gave his hand a sudden twist, and there was an ugly crunch of bones as Wesley's hand went limp, releasing the gun. Catwoman gave him a brutal knee to the face, and he collapsed, unconscious.

Kicking his gun away, Catwoman melted into the shadows. *One down*, she thought, *two to go*.

Tracing the sounds of the scuffle, Laurel and Armando found Wesley a moment later. Laurel motioned for Armando to double back to the front of the storage space. She would handle the rear.

As Armando skulked toward the front of the space, he noticed a spot of dark liquid on the floor. Kneeling down, he ran his finger through the liquid. Blood. There were more drops nearby, running in what appeared to be a trail.

Armando followed the blood. He was sure it would lead him to the injured cop.

He followed the droplets to a billboard smeared with blood—the one that Lone had leaned against. He eyed the streak of blood, following it to Lone's dark hiding space. Quickly, Armando leaned down to face Lone, gun drawn.

But Lone wasn't there.

Armando turned just in time to see Lone's fist connect with his jaw. Reeling, Armando lost his gun, and Lone took his opportunity. Lowering his good shoulder, Lone slammed Armando back against the billboard.

Armando tried to recover, but Lone caught him with a roundhouse punch, dropping him to the floor. Armando was out cold.

Lone sank to his knees. That had been all he could manage.

He just hoped it was enough.

Meanwhile, Laurel crept through the dark passageways bearing her image, sighting down the barrel of her gun. But she didn't see Catwoman, who was settled lightly atop a billboard of Laurel's eye.

Laurel took another step. Then two. When she was directly under the billboard, Catwoman gave the billboard a kick, knocking the heavy panel toward Laurel. Laurel dived away just in time—the panel missed her. Catwoman leaped to the floor.

Laurel caught sight of Catwoman's sparkling claws before her. Leveling her gun, Laurel fired, punching a hole in one of her own paper faces. Catwoman had been too quick. Laurel caught a movement out of the corner of her eye and fired again, mowing down her own cutouts. More rounds landed in posters and billboards, always missing the black clad figure that darted shadowlike through the darkness.

The figure disappeared, and Laurel held her fire. She paused for a moment, keeping perfectly still. There it was—a movement, above her. Looking up, Laurel saw Catwoman scaling the upper rail of a catwalk.

Claws extended, Catwoman leaped just as Laurel let loose another round.

Bam! Bam! Bam!

Catwoman twisted in the air, somersaulting away from the bullets, and collided with Laurel, sending them both crashing to the floor. Rolling away from Laurel, Catwoman rose to face her enemy.

But not in time.

Laurel was staring at her down the barrel of a gun. With a nasty grin, Laurel pulled the trigger.

Click.

The gun was empty.

Tossing aside the pistol, Laurel squared off to face Catwoman—the woman of stone against the woman of feline grace. Laurel attacked, locking arms with Catwoman and sending them rolling across the floor. Using their momentum, Laurel sent Catwoman spinning, then unleashed a hail of blows, driving Catwoman back toward the bank of windows. Laurel jumped after her, attacking with an intensity that bordered on madness. Catwoman stayed cool, dodging blow after blow and attacking with her claws. But she didn't do much damage, aside from shredding Laurel's clothes.

"I can't be hurt," Laurel said with a sneer.

"Beau-line," Catwoman snarled.

"Sure, if you stop taking it, your face disintegrates," Laurel said. "But if you keep taking it, you become as perfect as me. Skin like living marble, and you can't feel a thing." With that, Laurel landed a vicious blow that sent Catwoman sailing into a large cluster of machinery. The jagged metal from the protruding pipes tore at Catwoman's skin, and she let out a yowl.

Blood flowed from a gash in Catwoman's leg. She tried to get to her feet, but it was useless. She curled her injured leg like a wounded animal. "I can't believe women ever looked up to you,"

Catwoman said, blood trickling from her lips. "You're a façade. A lie."

Laurel grabbed Catwoman by the head and threw her backward.

Injured, Catwoman backed away. Laurel's strength was greater than she had imagined.

Sensing the kill, Laurel stalked her prey. "And what are you?" she growled. "A hero?" Laurel slammed Catwoman again, sending her writhing against the floor in pain. "A thief?" Laurel suggested. "A freak? If you don't have an identity, why keep it a secret?"

My identity, Catwoman thought, looking up at Laurel. In a flash, she remembered Patience—herself. *How did I get here?* Patience wondered. Whether in answer to Laurel's question or her own, Catwoman replied, "Because you killed me. You flushed me down the pipes that night. I'm Patience Philips." *I am Patience Philips*, Catwoman thought, feeling disoriented.

Laurel's eyes grew wide. "It was you—" she demanded. "The mousy girl from the art department? That's who's under there?"

Fear struck into the depths of Patience's

heart. *Laurel's right,* she thought. *I'm just a girl who likes to paint. I don't know how to fight!*

Laurel grabbed a metal pipe and gave it a violent swing, slamming Catwoman in the head. Catwoman rolled backward toward the bank of windows. Blood streamed from the wound in her head.

"I get it," Laurel growled. "You're just a scared little girl playing dress-up."

Catwoman grunted as Laurel kicked her with a pointed boot.

"A nobody," Laurel snapped. "A nothing."

Another of Laurel's kicks sent Catwoman against the angled window. Catwoman slammed facedown against the glass, beaten.

"Lucky for me, everyone thinks you're a psycho killer," Laurel went on. "It won't be a surprise when they find out you killed a cop."

A cop. Lone. The thought stopped Catwoman cold. She looked up, her eyes narrowing. Rage flowed through her body and her claws tightened.

"Aww . . ." Laurel said, reading the fury on Catwoman's face. "You want to save him?" Her voice was as hard as metal. "Honey, you can't even save yourself. The game's over."

She swung the wooden bar against the glass. Shattering, it began to give way beneath Catwoman. It was thirty stories to the street below.

Not now, Catwoman realized. *I can't give up now. I may be Patience Philips, but I'm also Catwoman . . . and I can't let Laurel win*. She looked at Laurel, her eyes glittering with cold ferocity. *This game isn't over until I say it is*, she thought. "We're going into overtime," Catwoman announced.

Just then, the glass gave way beneath her, and Catwoman leaped into the air—to the ceiling, twenty feet above. Hanging from a support strut, Catwoman glared down at Laurel, then leaped, twisting and landing on all fours in front of Laurel.

"One thing you'll never get, Laurel," Catwoman said, staring down the former model, "beauty isn't only skin deep." Then Catwoman let out a wild roar. The primal sound continued to echo through to the storage space as she leaped, slamming into Laurel and sending both of them rolling. Struggling, Laurel managed to break free, but Catwoman snapped her whip and pulled Laurel back into the fight.

Catwoman fought like a demon, her eyes glinting dangerously. For the first time, Laurel began to look frightened as Catwoman unleashed a furious attack. Reaching out, Catwoman slashed Laurel across the face, imbedding her claws in the live marble of Laurel's skin and sending her spinning. There was an eerie cracking sound as Laurel staggered away.

Catwoman clawed at Laurel again and the skin of Laurel's face cracked like broken glass. She staggered backward toward the windows.

"No!" Laurel screamed.

Quick as lightning, Catwoman cracked her whip, wrapping it around Laurel's wrist and stopping her fall.

Laurel looked down at the street far below. "Please," she begged as she began to slip backward, "Help me. Don't let me fall."

Catwoman looked at Laurel's ruined beauty

—her fractured face—and remembered that she had once been kind to Patience. "I may not be a hero," Catwoman admitted, "but I'm not a killer. And I want everyone to see you for what you really are," Catwoman added as she hauled Laurel back into the building

But as Laurel rose toward the windows, she caught sight of her own reflection in the shattered glass.

"No," Laurel whispered in horror. "I'm not perfect anymore." She touched her face with one hand, running her fingers across the cracked flesh. The other hand barely held on to Catwoman's whip. As Laurel tried to hang on in her intense shock, the whip began to fray, splintered by the shards of broken glass. Then suddenly—*SNAP!*—the whip broke apart.

"Laurel!" Catwoman screamed.

Laurel felt the floor slip beneath her feet. Terrified, she scrambled for the whip, but its remains snaked through her grasp.

Catwoman reached for Laurel, but she was too late. Laurel fell backward into the darkness, plummeting to her death.

When Laurel hit the ground, she shattered like a marble statue.

Patience stared down at the street sadly. She knew that there had been some good in Laurel . . . but in the end, her vanity was too powerful. *All the king's horses and all the king's men*, Patience thought sadly as she watched a crowd gather around Laurel, below.

There was a shuffling sound behind Patience as Lone walked up behind her.

"At least now they know the truth," Catwoman said. *Even if it came at a terrible price*, she added mentally. She turned to face him.

"I saw what you did," Lone told her. "You tried to save her."

A flicker of a smile played on Catwoman's lips. "Surprised?"

"No." Lone's voice was quiet. "Not at all."

Patience looked into Lone's eyes and saw the same kindness she had seen the first day she met him. The day he had saved her.

"You know," Lone said slowly, "if Patience is back in her cell tomorrow morning, it would be awfully tough to prove she was Catwoman."

"Like I said," Catwoman replied, "I'm a lucky girl."

"No," Lone corrected, smiling, "you said Patience was a lucky girl."

"Exactly." Catwoman kissed Lone, and it was a kiss that held all of Catwoman's passion and Patience's love. It was a kiss that felt like a new beginning.

The moment it was over, Catwoman slipped into the darkness.

Lone watched her go.

Epilogue

Patience strolled through the art gallery, marveling at how far she had come. The gallery featured a special exhibition showcasing new artists, Patience among them. Proudly, she surveyed one of her paintings hanging on a wall.

Deep in thought, Patience didn't notice the person standing behind her.

"I spotted this artist a long time ago," a male voice said. "Before she got famous."

Patience turned to see Lone. She grinned. Just then Sally swooped in, carrying cocktails.

"Best cosmos in town," said Sally. "Extra everything. I'm supervising. And I am out of here."

As she walked away, Lone thanked Sally for the drink, then immediately handed it to another gallery guest—a cop is always on duty.

Relieved of the cocktail, Tom turned to Patience, with hints of both pride and hurt in his eyes.

"Congratulations, Patience. I'm really proud of you."

"Thanks," Patience replied. "That means a lot to me, coming from you." She was well aware of the pain she had caused the nice-guy cop.

"I'm sorry about..." Patience started.

Lone interrupted. "I know you think it could never work out with us."

Patience was not sure at first what to say. After all, just a short time ago she was a shy, insecure woman on the fast-track to nowhere. Now she was living her dream as an artist and having her work showcased in one of the city's most well-respected galleries.

"I'm not saying never, Tom," Patience responded. "But I've just figured out who—or what—I am, and I'm not so sure I can be her with you. Or if it would be fair to you, to even try."

Lone nodded, processing what had just been shared.

The pair looked deep into each others' eyes, both wishing that things could be different. Then Lone smiled, taking Patience's hand in his.

"If you change your mind, you know where to find me," he said.

Then, with a quizzical look, he gently touched one of the sparkling diamond earrings in her ears. He leaned in to give Patience a kiss, one both gentle and bittersweet.

Winking at Patience, Lone smiled. "Don't do anything I wouldn't do," he added.

Then Lone walked away, out of the gallery, and possibly out of Patience's life. She watched wistfully.

Just then a snooty art-world type walked up.

"I see such animalistic power in your work," the art patron said. "Such strength in the brush strokes, confidence in the color palette. You have a bright future ahead of you."

"Thanks," replied Patience. "I think I agree."

Then Patience walked through the crowd, her confidence exuding in her Catwoman strut.

Ophelia, off in a corner, looked on. She beamed as Midnight purred, perched up on Ophelia's shoulder.

HERE KITTY KITTY